Trapped In

Marquez Pritchett

This book is a work of fiction. It is a product of the author's imagination. Any similarity to actual events is purely coincidental.

CLF Publishing, LLC.
9161 Sierra Ave, Ste. 203C
Fontana, CA 92335
www.clfpublishing.org

Dedications

To my mother, Margie Pritchett, for loving me and encouraging me to keep God first in my life and to always remember anything is possible!

To my father, Richard Johnson, for believing in me and supporting me to follow my dreams, as well as embracing my ambition.

To my children, MarQue'sia and Marquez Pritchett, I love and adore you so very much.

Additionally, I dedicate this book to all the 'Aces' out there who are "Trapped In" and trying to get out.

I

Some folks say your life flashes before your eyes when your time is about to expire from this human existence. I never understood how that saying came to be because only those who crossed over would know. But, the phrase finally made sense when crimson liquid soaked through my wife beater t-shirt. All I could think of was life and why it turned out like this.

At that moment, I thought about my son growing up without his dad around, and I wondered if I would have another chance to teach him how to be a real man. I loved him to pieces, but his mom liked to make things hard, so we did not get the chance to genuinely bond like a father and son should. Joy did everything in her power to try and get full custody of Jr. in response to our failed relationship. She lashed out on what seemed like a daily basis.

"You love these streets more than you love me," she would say. Little did she know, everything I did was for her and my son.

The thoughts that entered my head were not flashes at all. They were elaborate memories of a past that I often tried to forget. My mind wandered as I lay there on the fresh blood-stained pavement unable to move an inch in any direction. The burning sensation poured through my limp body, and I avoided the light until the flashing red and white bulbs arrived.

A small crowd flocked to the scene and surrounded me in spite of the heavy summer rain that fell through humid skies. An old woman wearing a nightgown and headscarf prayed over me. Her words were soothing, even though I couldn't remember the last time I was in church. I doubted that she could save me, but my appreciation for the old lady's gesture was real. One of the onlookers was kind enough to cover my face with her coat until the ambulance came and collected me. The city's finest rounded the corner as the ambulance pulled off. They love to make a dramatic late entrance during these types of parties.

I go by the name of Ace, but my government name is Amir Johnson. Only Nana and Poppa call me Amir. Some of my friends don't even know that name exists, and I plan on keeping it that way. Hearing that name brings back some unsettling memories of my mom. I can still hear her voice now, "Amir, come eat, love bug." Words cannot describe how much I miss Mom's cooking. No matter how hard I try, I just can't get my pancakes to taste like hers.

Mom was always trying to protect me from the neighborhood I grew up in. No son of hers would become another product of the ghetto if it were up to her. She tried hard to shelter me, but I guess Mom was dealing with the same things she was protecting me from because she's been gone for a long time now. She was trapped in *that place;* at least that's what Nana called it.

Back then, Mom would sometimes leave for days at a time, and I had to stay with Nana and Poppa. And when I was home, our phone would ring at all times of the night. I grew older and began to understand that my mom was only doing what she had to do to keep a roof over our head. She just got caught up in the process.

My dad, on the other hand, retired himself from fatherhood duty when I was just a kid. At that age, I thought something was wrong with me because he hardly came around after he broke up with Mom. For years, I blamed myself for my parent's divorce. Eventually, I realized my dad is just an asshole, and life is probably better off without him. Last I knew, he was living on the east coast, and I have a little brother that I've never met.

After Mom was taken away, I became that young cat who always hung around the older crowd. Poppa and Nana became my stone, but I was still an unruly adolescent whenever they turned a blind eye towards me. Coping was hard without Mom around, but the time had come to either remain a child or step up to the plate to become a man. My story was just beginning, and I promised myself I wouldn't stop until my goal of becoming my own man was accomplished. Nothing and no one could stand in my way. I had come a long way to become the person I was, but I'll admit that there is still a lot of work to be done.

The bumpy ambulance ride kept me distracted from the intense pain that pierced my flesh. As the paramedics tried to stop the bleeding from the open wounds in my stomach and chest, I gritted my teeth so hard I chipped off part of a tooth. *Twenty-seven years on Earth and this is how it all ends?* I asked myself. I stared into the ambulance cab lights, and my thoughts took me back to the days when I used to be a *git*. That's just another way of saying *little boy*.

I was always the quiet one, and I kept to

myself; I hated that part of me. I am thankful that it was just a phase, so now I embrace that part of my past because that is how I adjusted after Mom left. Being content with my situation was essential before I could open up to the world again. Trust was something I didn't have a lot of. Today, I still don't.

Poppa and Nana did their best at raising me, but they were barely keeping their head above water with just the two of them. We never went hungry, but I knew my grandparents were struggling to make ends meet. Nana was a sweet little lady who had a way of sugarcoating everything. I guess that was her way of shielding me from reality. Sometimes, I would hear her praying for help late at night when she thought I was in bed. Nana would sit and braid her long silky hair and sing songs of inspiration until she fell asleep on the couch with the TV watching her. Nana was only looking out for my best interest, but I was well aware of our status, so I took it upon myself to do something about it.

My grandfather was the total opposite of my grandma. He knew what I was up to, so I couldn't get over on him for nothing. Poppa would always ask me, "Why, Amir? Why?" Something about Poppa made me feel at ease when conversing with him, but he still got me where it hurt. Grandpa stayed on my case, and I love him for that. "No matter what you do, Amir, there will always be consequences waiting."

Poppa was a massive ebony man who spoke in a calm but firm tone. To this day, Grandpa's baritone voice is always in the back of my head before I make a stupid decision. Poppa always kept it real. He even told me, "Out of all of your friends, James, is the real one. Keep him close."

James Hurtch lived in the same neighborhood as my grandparents and was the type of kid that was well rounded, into sports, and educated. He was always the talented one and was the brains of all my friends, even though he was two years younger than I was. James was my right hand man and like a brother from another mother. He was on his way to meet me right before things went wrong, and I ended up in the back of an ambulance. That was the one time I was grateful for traffic because James would have been in the ambulance with me, or worse.

My vision was dimming, and I began to go in and out of consciousness when the paramedics finally delivered me to the emergency room. I heard a nurse talking to the medics and her pen taping her clipboard as she wrote down details. The nurse asked me, "What is your name, sir?" No sound escaped when I tried to answer her. Life was rapidly draining from me. For the first time in a long time, I felt helplessness and fear. Those were the emotions I suppressed when my goals became my first priority.

Maybe that was my problem: I was all about the dollar signs. There was only one goal in mind at the time, and I constantly repeated it to remain on track: "You will become a successful businessman." Somewhere along the way, I lost focus of my path, and I let the game get the best of me, but I knew I was better than that.

Mixing personal and business life tends to complicate things, but both aspects of my life are important to me and somewhere along the way they became intertwined. Soon my business life became personal, and my personal life was consumed with business. The people in my personal life suffered because I treated them like another facet of business and often put family on the backburner to focus on making my money grow.

Business also suffered when it became personal and associates turned into enemies overnight. The more powerful I became, the more opportunities I had to make decisions based off personal vendettas. So if I didn't like you, I wouldn't fuck with you. Period. That's what happens when egos get the best of you, and the little people who helped along the way get stepped on.

The fluorescent bulbs on the ceiling streaked by as my gurney was rushed to an operating room. My mother suddenly crossed my mind when we pushed through the automatic sliding doors. I thought about her often, but this was the first time that there was a possibility that I may not see her again. The thought alone caused a clear salty liquid to roll out of the corner of my eye. I hadn't cried since my mother was gone, and I wasn't about to start.

The realization was harsh because I hadn't seen Mom since my twelfth birthday. That was the same day the law came to take her away. My birthdays hadn't been the same since. A phone conversation was the closest I had been to my mom in fifteen years.

When I sent in a request for visitation, she rejected me. "I don't want you to see me caged up like some animal, Amir," Mom had said, trying to explain her reasoning. As a child, that made me feel inferior, so I was angry and didn't talk to her for five years straight. As a man, I understand my mom's reasons for not letting me visit her. But as her only child, I would have given anything to see her before

I took my last breath.

The operating room was colder than the rest of the hospital, or maybe I was just starting to lose warmth from the lack of blood flowing in my system. An attractive female surgeon wearing specs with her hair in a bun made her way over to me and introduced herself as she gave me a once over and snapped on a pair of latex gloves.

"Hello Mr. Johnson. I'm Dr. Bryant, your surgeon. Don't try to speak. If you can hear me, blink twice fast."

I somehow managed to blink twice. Then, I tried to keep my lids open long enough to take in the eye candy in case it was my last. Dr. Bryant warmly put a hand on my shoulder and replied, "Okay, Mr. Johnson. You've suffered multiple gunshot wounds, so we have to perform emergency surgery. We're going to put you under anesthesia, so you won't feel anything until you wake up. Just try to stay calm, and let us take care of you."

A hulk-like male nurse stood over me and placed a mask over my nose and mouth as the team rushed to prepare for surgery. "Mr. Johnson, I want you to count backwards starting from one hundred." The nurse's demeanor was flamboyant despite his intimidating mien. The countdown from one hundred started, but I didn't remember getting past ninety when I slipped away into a state of unconsciousness.

When the lids of my eyes cracked open again, I tried to focus my blurry vision around the room. Monitors attached to me beeped rhythmically. Someone was sitting next to my bed, but I couldn't make out exactly whom the person was. I squinted and peered through the dim light to get a better look. "Hey, you're up," the person said. The voice was familiar, but I still wasn't sure who was there.

The shadowy figure stood up and walked towards my bed into the light. "Mom!" I tried to yell, but it was more of a harsh whisper. Mom was there in my hospital room. I didn't understand it, and I didn't even care as I grasped on to her like white on rice.

This time, I was not going to let go as the tears freely flowed from my eyes.

"Oh, Amir. I've missed you so much, love bug. What are you doing in here, baby? You had me so worried. We thought we were gonna lose you last night." Her voice was shaky and desperate. Mom held me so tightly it hurt.

"Mom, wait I'm still healing." I had forgotten I was fresh out of surgery.

The excitement in her made me smile. As she held me tighter and tighter, the pain shot through me.

"Hold up, Mom. You're hurting me." The grasp got even tighter, and I panicked. I felt the wetness of fresh blood seep through the gauzes.

"Mom, what are you doing? Stop!" I pleaded as I weakly struggled to release myself from her hold. Confusion ran through my head when I yelled out in agony, "Why are you doing this?" Blood was starting to soak through my patient garments as she slightly released her hold enough to look at me in the eyes.

Chills traveled through my spine when I saw my mom's eyes were suddenly pitch black and big as an owl's.

"I love you, Amir. I would never hurt you." Her lips formed an evil smirk. Then, she wrapped her hands around my throat after I screamed for the nurse.

Two nurses entered the room. As I struggled to breathe, Mom let go of my neck. The nurses' scrubs were all black, and they had black masks over their faces and black latex gloves on their hands. My wounds were bleeding heavily. I peeled back my saturated garments and revealed several quarter-sized black holes in my torso, but I saw no blood. *Huh? Where was the blood coming from?* I thought. My mind couldn't comprehend it.

When I looked up, Mom's shirt was drenched in red as she turned to the nurses and prepared to lunge just as one of them pulled out a Beretta with a silencer attached. Mom disregarded the pistol and lunged anyway as the nurse pulled the trigger. I cried out as the bullet traveled through my mom's head. Her body dropped lifelessly on the linoleum floor.

"What have you done?" I pleaded for answers.

The nurses remained silent as they stood over my mom's body to shoot her again. I looked away unable to do anything to stop them. Footsteps click clacked towards me until I felt the heat from the barrel of the silencer next to my ear. I slowly turned causing the nurse's gun to press into my cheek. She peered into my soul when we made eye contact. Her eyes were empty and emotionless, cold as snow. After a few moments, the nurse backed away with her gun still trained on me. *Why?* I thought.

The question would go unanswered as the nurse let off another round and the flash of light jolted my body awake. I gasped for air and almost choked on the plastic tube in my throat that was helping me breathe. The room was the same, but no one was sitting beside me as I scanned my surroundings.

It was just a nightmare and my heart

rate slowed back down to a normal pace while I attempted to make sense of what had just happened. I couldn't wrap my mind around the dream or what it meant. All I knew was it felt too real, and I never wanted to have another dream like it.

As the anxiety faded away, the pain from the wounds hit me like a ton of bricks. My groaning made a nurse rush into the room to see what was happening.

"Up already? I'm surprised. You're a real fighter, Mr. Johnson. We almost lost you in there. Strong boy you are."

The elderly nurse spoke gently with a Caribbean accent as she checked the monitors behind my bed. "I'm going to give you something for the pain. I know you need it."

I looked up as the nurse injected the I.V. line with a dose of morphine. The medicine flowed quickly through my veins as I felt an instant numbness, and I succumbed to the pain. The nurse checked my bandages and ordered me to get some rest, as if I really had a choice.

The early morning sunlight penetrated the slightly opened blinds when I woke to greet the day. The tube was out of my throat, and I was breathing on my own. I waited for the sunrays to reach me as I watched them inch closer with every second that passed. The warmth of the sun was so simple but so sweet at the same time.

"How did you sleep? We thought you were in a coma for a minute there," the elderly nurse said as she made her way into the room.

My voice cracked from the dryness in my throat, "How long was I out?"

"Well, let's just say I didn't know if you were sleeping or hibernating," she giggled as she changed my IV bag. "The doctor will be in to see you shortly. Oh, I almost forgot you had a visitor: your brother. He waited here for hours while you were sleeping. He just got on the elevator. Let me call the lobby to see if security can catch him."

The nurse bolted out of the room before I could say anything. *Brother?* I thought to myself. Nobody knew I was in the hospital, so that didn't make any sense, and the only brother I had was one I never met. *Who could be claiming to be my brother to visit me if no one knows I'm even here?* I thought to myself. The dream about my mom crossed my mind, and concern about the mystery visitor and his intentions were strong.

"My nigga!" The door flew open and startled me as I looked over to see who my brother was. In walked Black, a hefty dark-skinned dude with a smile stretched across his face. Black is my other brother from another mother. He has enough personality to let you borrow some of it and not have to ask for any of it back. Nobody understood how he was able to get so many girls because he was big, ugly, and black as charcoal. What people failed to understand was the fact that he had what most of these cats out here don't have these days: heart. Not just heart, but a heart of gold.

Black is a protector by nature. We met when I was new to my grandparents' neigh-borhood and got jacked for my bike by a couple of punks who lived on the other side of town. One of the punks steered, and one rode the handlebars, but they didn't get far down the block before Black came out of nowhere and kicked the bike over into the street. Black snatched the bike back and threatened them with his appearance. The way those punks ran home crying is one of the funniest sights I have ever seen.

"Next time, you gonna have to pay me to get this shit back, lil' homie. I should keep it for myself but it would prolly' bend like a paperclip if I get on it." Black never missed an opportunity to crack a joke. We've been tight ever since that day.

"I knew you had a lil' Tupac in you, Ace." Black walked over and grabbed a hold of my hand to give me a proper greeting.

"How did you know I was in here?" The sound that left my mouth was barely audible.

"My triple ex-girlfriend works in the ER now. She said she saw your name on the patient list when she got to work this morning. I shot over here as soon as she called." Black's tone was always set to *outside voice*. "Look, I know you need time to heal up, but you better do it like Wolverine fast. We got work to put in. Ain't nobody gonna try to put my family in the dirt and walk away clean like…" Black was interrupted by a clearing throat behind him. Dr. Bryant stood in the doorway.

"Good morning, Mr. Johnson. You gave us quite a scare the other night. You're lucky to be alive, sir. We revived you twice on the operating table."

Black's eyes went wide; then, he mouthed the word "DAMN!" to me when Dr. Bryant walked by. She was truly an angel, my angel.

"You are a miracle worker, Doc. I can't thank you enough for saving my life." I was being modest. Dr. Bryant grabbed some latex gloves from the nearby sink counter after washing her hands.

"Don't thank me, Mr. Johnson. Thank God. I'm just a very small part of the bigger picture." Doc refused to take all of the credit.

Dr. Bryant reclined my bed back to the flat position, "Ok, we're going to run a few tests to determine your recovery, Mr. Johnson. One of the bullets clipped your vertebrae, which caused a minor fracture. The bullet came very close to your spinal cord, but we could not find any structural harm to the spinal canal."

Black couldn't help but to blurt out, "I'm next."

Dr. Bryant smiled, "I wasn't planning on doing any prostate exams today, but sure I can fit you in somewhere."

Black's expression shifted from pleasant to distraught, "Did I say I'm next? I meant I'm texting again. New phone."

Dr. Bryant chuckled, "Sir, I'm going to have to ask you to leave the room while I perform the exam." No way could I let that happen.

"He can stay. I want him to stay. He's family." The doctor nodded and respected my wishes.

Dr. Bryant placed her stethoscope on

my chest and asked me to breathe deeply. Sharp pains struck me with each breath. Dr. Bryant noticed me wincing and took note. Then, she instructed, "Wiggle your fingers for me." Not only did I wiggle my fingers, I lifted my arms and wiggled them too. Doc laughed at my antics, "Ok, now wiggle your toes for me, Mr. Johnson."

I interrupted her for a simple request, "You can call me, Ace, Doc. Everybody calls me, Ace."

Dr. Bryant nodded her head, "Ok, Ace. Wiggle your toes." After a few moments, Dr. Bryant repeated herself, "You said Ace right? Wiggle your toes for me."

"I'm trying." The task seemed foreign as I focused my mind intensely on my lower half.

Dr. Bryant put pressure on my feet and asked, "Can you feel that?" I shook my head "no." The doctor repositioned her hands and asked again, "How about that? Do you feel anything at all?" I shook my head "no" again.

Dr. Bryant let out a long sigh and pulled

her gloves off as she sat in a chair next to my bed. Her spirits noticeably deflated as she picked up her clipboard. Doc didn't have to say a word for me to realize what was happening, so I cut right in before she tried to explain, "How bad is it, Doc?"

Dr. Bryant removed her specs and took a moment to collect her thoughts before she replied, "We thought the bullet missed your spine, as there were no signs of injury. The bullet could have grazed against your spinal cord, but the x-rays do not reveal serious damage."

"How bad is it?" I asked again.

Delivering that type of news was difficult for Dr. Bryant because she struggled to say, "I'm sorry, Ace. You are paralyzed from the waist down."

Black couldn't help but to react angrily to the news, "Damn! Paralyzed? He's going to walk again. Right, Doc? He's gonna be back on his feet in no time, right?"

Dr. Bryant didn't want to get ahead of herself, but she answered anyway, "I can't tell you if it is temporary or permanent. We have to run a few more tests before we can determine Ace's chances at recovering mobility in his legs. Only time will tell."

II

The glow from the television dimly illuminated the hospital room as I lay there staring blankly at a muted late night program. An infomercial tried to convince me to buy some crap I didn't need, but none of the images on the screen registered in my brain. My mind was stuck in a trance, still trying to process everything that happened in the past couple of days. I asked Black to get in touch with my grandparents because they were still unaware that I was in the hospital, but I told him not to tell them what Dr. Bryant said about my recovery. Nana had a weak heart already, and she could only take so much stress at one time.

I felt more vulnerable lying there than I ever had in my unpredictable life. The feeling was reminiscent to the day Mom was taken away by the law and my whole world was turned upside down.

Mom had made my favorite for dinner that night: mac and cheese. I was so excited I went straight for the first bite without giving thanks, and Mom popped the fork out of my hand and said, "Did you bless your food, Amir?"

Mom never let me get away without saying a prayer before, but it was my twelfth birthday, and I thought I was grown enough to decide not to. The rebellion didn't last long; I mumbled a prayer and immediately got skinny eyes from Mom as she scrunched her eyelids and looked at me with a final warning.

The words came out clear the next time, "Lord, bless this food that we are about to receive, and for my beautiful mother who cooked it. Amen!" Without wasting another second, I dug into the food like a nutritionally-deprived beast.

Mom smiled and said, "Slow down, Amir. The plate won't grow legs anytime soon."

After devouring my dinner, Mom reached under the tablecloth and brought out a gift box wrapped in shiny blue paper and handed it to me, "Happy birthday, love bug. I got something special for you." My face lit up, and I darted over to Mom and hugged her tightly.

I whispered, "Thanks, Mom."

Mom chuckled and said, "You don't even know what it is yet! Open it."

When I made the first tear in the wrapping paper, the front door to our apartment was violently rammed across the living room, breaking the porcelain vase on the coffee table. A loud bang pierced my ear drums as smoke consumed the room, as uninvited men in black tactical gear invaded our apartment with their assault rifles drawn.

"Police Department," they yelled.

Mom screamed and put her hands up. One of the officers quickly cuffed her and led her out of the apartment. Another officer grabbed ahold of me when I tried to go after Mom and said, "Calm down, buddy. Everything is going to be okay." Somehow, I managed to squirm my way out of his grasp to run outside just before Mom was put into the backseat of an unmarked cruiser. No sound came from Mom's voice from behind the window, but I saw her mouth the words, "Don't cry, love bug. I'll be okay."

The sound of someone knocking on my hospital room door brought me back to reality. I looked up to see Nana, Poppa, and Black walk in together. Nana cried out and put her hands over her mouth in disbelief.

With tears in her eyes, she said, "What did they do to my baby?" Nana approached my bed and kissed me on my forehead. "We haven't seen you in weeks, Amir. That's not how you do the people you love."

Poppa was noticeably angry; he was breathing heavily and holding a clinched fist. "Who did this to you, Amir? How did this happen?"

Black jumped in and replied before I could, "We got it under control. Whoever did this to Ace is going to get the favor returned." Poppa knew exactly what that meant.

"Don't do nothing stupid, Black. Just be thankful Amir wasn't killed. Let the law and karma take care of 'em. You don't want to end up in prison or dead. Sometimes, you gotta count your blessings."

Even if Black wanted to retaliate, we couldn't. I had no idea who shot me or the motive behind their actions. I admit I had created a few enemies in the past, but I didn't think I had the kind that would want me dead. Guess I thought wrong. Anyone is capable.

Nana stood beside my bed and held my hand. The energy in the room was somber, but overall, we were appreciative of the chance to have that moment together. Nana never stopped babying me, even though I was old enough to do things for myself. That's just who Nana was. There were times when I wished she wouldn't treat me like a baby, but those feelings weren't there that day. Being able to spend another day with family made me more than grateful, and Nana's touch eased some of my worry.

Suddenly, I felt like a kid again, and nostalgia for the days that were less complicated set in. I realized the trials I faced while growing up were a cakewalk compared to what I had encountered in my adult life.

Everything changed when Mom left. When I went to live with my grandparents, I went into a dark place mentally, and it took a long time to open up to anyone again. Nana and Poppa were there for me and did everything they could to help me deal with the loss, but for some reason I still lashed out and did things that I would have never thought of if Mom were around. Even when I was aware that I was being mischievous, I still did wrong because it helped me release some of the pent-up anger.

My grandparents didn't understand

what had gotten into me. They always considered me to be a good kid, and even after I started to act out of the ordinary, they still treated me like one. Poppa knew I was going through a phase and punishing me was not enough because it never changed the way I felt inside. Often times, a punishment would make my attitude worse, and I resented my grandparents for trying to raise me right. There came a point when I shut my grandparents out because I felt like they really didn't understand. They tried everything in the book to reach me but didn't know how to get through the walls I had built up.

Eventually, my behavior grew worse when Poppa and I started to clash because he was running out of ways to punish me. One night, I came home hours after curfew because James and I had skipped school and spent the day at the beach to enjoy the scenery and nonchalantly stare at half-naked women.

Poppa had never raised his voice before, so I could tell he had enough of my foolishness because he yelled at me, "You think this is some kind of game, Amir? If your mom were around, you would never act like this. I'm gonna let you do some thinking tonight and maybe you will come to appreciate what you have here and learn to respect your elders. We want you here, but you don't have to be here, Amir."

Poppa was so angry he made me sleep on the porch without dinner. Naturally, my blood boiled, and I became angry with Poppa for scorning me, but nothing he said made any difference in my behavior. The only thing Poppa did at the time was make me hate him for bringing up my mother.

The temperatures dropped and the air became frigid after a couple of hours sitting on the porch fuming with a bad attitude. I decided to take a walk to warm up when I noticed the garage door was accidently left open with just enough space for me to squeeze under, so I slid inside the opening to escape my punishment.

A load of clothes spinning in the dryer provided relief from the cold as my shivering body absorbed the heat. There was an old couch in the garage that I could sleep on. It wasn't my bed, but it would do for a night. Poppa collected a variety of sports memorabilia, and I loved to gaze at the posters of legends on the walls. Sometimes, I would mimic the athletes' poses on the posters and imagine how it would be to be them. Poppa would go on and on about how the athletes from his day played with heart and how athletes today just want the spotlight.

Poppa never let me touch any of the collectables. He would probably throw a fit if I came within inches of physical contact of the exhibit. Almost everything in the garage was off limits to me, but when I noticed the lock on the steel cabinet that Poppa prohibited me from was left open, temptation ran through me.

Stealthily, I removed the lock and put it in my jacket pocket while looking over my shoulder as a precaution. The hinges on the cabinet squeaked loudly when I tried to open the doors, so I swung them open swiftly to make it fast. The adrenaline quickened my heart rate. I paused momentarily to listen for footsteps, but only the TV was audible, so I proceeded to click on an overhead light bulb inside the cabinet.

Goosebumps covered my skin as I discovered Poppa's gun collection. If I were my grandfather, I wouldn't want to me to see that either. I questioned my stupidity, but there was no way I could go that far and stop. Besides, I just wanted to hold one of them. I reached for the chrome plated .38, the shiniest gun in the collection. The gun was heavy in my inexperienced, vibrating hands. Nerves made my heart produce the loudest sound in the house.

Holding the gun down on one side then the other, I posed in front of a mirror in the garage while mean mugging my reflection. I pointed the gun at the mirror and admired my tough guy look when something abruptly crashed on the garage floor and startled me. BANG! The gun went off and the bullet destroyed the mirror. A stray cat yelped and dashed for the exit.

My body froze like a popsicle, and my heart dropped into my stomach. Life as I knew it was about to be over. After the shock passed through me, I ran towards the cabinet and placed the gun back the way I found it and locked it up. Then, I slid under the garage door again for a clean getaway, but I ran directly into Poppa when I popped out from under the garage door opening.

Motionless, I stood there waiting for Poppa to lay his wrath upon me. I stared at the ground avoiding eye contact. A few seconds passed as Poppa looked at me expressionless. Then, without a word, he walked into the house without looking back. For the first time in a long time, I felt regret for my actions. My grandfather had finally given up on me.

When daybreak approached, my grandfather came out of the house fully dressed, holding a duffle bag and a metal briefcase. He gave me orders, "Difficult one, get in the truck." I was confused and a little scared because he still had not mentioned anything about the night before.

There were hardly any cars on the road as we pulled off towards the unknown destination. Poppa didn't say where we were going, and there was no way I was about to start questioning the man. We drove for a while, listening to jazz radio without exchanging any words. When Poppa is upset, he stays silent while thinking of the perfect way to express himself without letting anger get the best of him.

About a half hour into our trip, Poppa turned off the radio. He took a moment before asking me, "What do you think it takes to be a real man?"

I didn't know where he was going with that question, but I answered anyway, "Age. When you turn eighteen, you're a man."

Poppa didn't hesitate to reply, "Wrong! Try again. What does it take to be a man?"

I reluctantly gave another answer, "Being successful at life and making money. Real men make money, right?"

Poppa shook his head to disagree, "Wrong again, Amir. What else you got?"

The answer he was looking for was a little more complicated than expected.

I replied, "I got nothing."

We exited the highway and turned off onto a two-lane road and drove towards the mountains in the distance. Poppa continued to get his point across, "You don't know what it takes to be a real man, because nobody ever taught you what it means to be a real man, and that's not your fault. First and foremost, Amir, to be a real man you need to learn how to be selfless. A real man is not only concerned with the well-being of himself and understands that without the world around him, he is nobody. You can be the most incredible man to ever walk the Earth, but if no one acknowledges it, you are just like everyone else."

Poppa made me recognize how selfish I had been. The reasons I was always angry were selfish. I was constantly thinking about what I didn't have or what I lost and how it was affecting me. Never did it occur to me that I could easily let go of those selfish feelings.

The scenery was therapeutic. As we traveled up the curvy mountain road, the lake beneath us offered a mesmerizing performance of sunrays dancing on rippling water.

Poppa kept passing on wisdom while focusing on the narrow road, "A real man never lets his emotions control his actions. Letting someone get a reaction out of you gives him more control than you have over yourself. Emotions are temporary. Don't make impulsive decisions based on how someone else made you feel. Some people enjoy getting a reaction out of you for no reason at all, but don't let anyone provoke you. Talk is cheap."

I was guilty for feeding into negativity that came my way and letting situations get the best of me. I suddenly felt childish.

Poppa drove his truck off the main road and parked on the shoulder. He grabbed the duffle bag from the backseat; then, he gave me the briefcase to carry. The case was a little weighted, but I managed. Curiosity made me ask, "Poppa, what's in this case? It's kinda heavy."

Poppa smirked and said, "You'll find out soon enough."

The trail we followed was obviously not a popular one because the dense forest was hard to maneuver through. The heavy case made my fingers ache, and I constantly switched hands as we hiked through the unkempt trail deeper into the woods. Poppa walked behind me with the duffle bag strapped over his shoulder, watching me struggle with the case.

The hike was challenging, but Poppa kept talking, "Responsibility and account-ability is what a real man strives for each and every day. Not possessing these qualities and exercising them one hundred percent of the time causes people to lose belief in you, and anything you say or do will mean nothing. Real men never run from responsibility. We embrace it because that's what shapes our character and drive. Being able to focus on priorities is the key to success."

No one had ever taken the time to have that type of conversation with me. Poppa's words sank in deep as he added, "If you don't have your word, you don't have anything."

After hiking through the dense forest for about a mile and a half, we came upon a clearing where a creek directed fresh water down the mountainside. Poppa dropped the duffle bag and said, "We're here."

The briefcase was released from my hold, and I rubbed my red palms together to get the feeling back into my hands. Pinecones and dead leaves covered the forest floor. Three tree stumps near the creek were aligned almost perfectly a few feet apart from one another.

Poppa unzipped the duffle bag and pulled out three empty cans that once preserved some sort of vegetable and set one on top of each tree stump. Then, he walked over to put the combination into the briefcase. The latches flipped open, and Poppa opened the case to reveal a black hunting rifle.

He looked at me and said, "Since you're so curious about guns, I thought I might teach you a thing or two about them. What you did last night was irresponsible and stupid, but I didn't bring you here to punish you, Amir. I brought you here to open your eyes and help you see everything that you've been missing."

Poppa took the gun out of the case and loaded it with the ammunition he brought in the duffle bag. Then, he positioned himself about twenty yards away from the tree stumps on the other side of the clearing. Poppa told me to get behind him as he cocked the rifle and looked through the scope to aim at the cans on the tree stumps. BANG! Poppa knocked the first can off the tree stump and cocked the gun again. BANG! The second can dropped. Poppa cocked the rifle one more time and focused. BANG! The last and smallest can was taken out.

My mouth stretched down to my chest with disbelief. I had no idea my grandfather could shoot like that. The excitement made my voice squeak when I yelled, "Whoa, Poppa! Where did you learn how to do that?"

Poppa laughed and said, "Just a little something my father taught me. Now I'm going to teach you." Poppa knew this was the only way to reach me. Punishing me would have changed nothing.

As Poppa re-loaded the rifle, I replaced the cans on the stumps. Then, Poppa handed the rifle to me.

"Make sure you hold the butt of the gun against your shoulder. You don't want it to go flying backwards after you let a shot off. This baby has a lil' kick. The safety is right here next to the trigger. It's off right now. The other way is on. Go ahead. Put the gun up and look through the scope." Poppa handed me the loaded gun and took a step back. I held the rifle up to my shoulder and looked out of the scope with one eye squinted.

Poppa gave more direction, "Now you want your target to be in the middle of the cross on the scope. You see that?" I nodded my head yes, but it was hard to stay focused on the can as my hands shook uncontrollably from nerves.

My grandpa reassured me, "Take your time, Amir. When you're ready, pull the trigger and…" BANG! The rifle went off before he could finish, and my body flew backwards from the force of the gun as I took a few steps to regain my balance. Poppa laughed loudly and grabbed my shoulder. "She's got some power. Doesn't she boy? Cock it, and try again."

After shaking off the impact from the rifle, I took a few steps back to my original position and took a deep breath before cocking the gun and putting it back up to my shoulder. I took my time and aimed for the can. Then, I let off another shot. The target was unharmed again.

After several attempts at shooting the largest can, my shoulder began to hurt, and I dropped the gun. Poppa walked over to me and grabbed the rifle. He started to reload while I sulked. "I can't do it. It's too hard,

Poppa."

Poppa continued to reload, "What do you mean you can't do it? A real man never gives up. No matter what obstacle is set up in front of him he never gives up on something that he wants. Having that type of willpower with everything that you do will make you stronger than those who aren't willing to do what you will to get the job done. Those are the real winners in life. You tell me, are you a winner, or are you going to let life beat you out of what you really want?"

I looked up at Poppa towering over me as he held the rifle out for me to take. I took the gun from his grasp and took a few steps back to reposition myself in front of the tin cans. That time, I took a moment to focus and breathe before I put the gun up to aim again. When I felt confident enough, I aimed at the can and let off another round. The target still went untouched.

Poppa clapped his hands and kept encouraging me. "That's okay, son. Keep trying; you almost got it." I cocked the gun again and gritted my teeth. My determination increased. My focus was not shaky anymore as I was in tune with every muscle in my body and kept the gun trained.

Just as I started to put pressure on the trigger, a low growl coming from the bushes behind us made me halt. I snatched the gun down and turn around to see what was threatening us. Poppa turned just as a full-grown cougar leaped over the bushes and landed directly in front of him.

The ferocious cat squared up with Poppa. The deep growl made me tremble as it flashed its razor sharp teeth at my grandfather. Its muscles flexed underneath its fur ready to pounce at a moment's notice. Poppa drew his hunting blade from the holster and crouched low, as he slowly backed away. Poppa was a large man, but the cougar wasn't intimidated. It crept closer, growling as Poppa backed away.

Without taking his eyes off of the cougar, Poppa stayed low and talked to me. "Amir, I need to you to focus. You only got one shot, okay?" Poppa kept backing up, and I trained my gun on the cougar as it crept forward towards him. Sweat rolled down his forehead, but he remained in defense mode. The cat crept closer keeping eye contact with Poppa.

Then, it suddenly pounced at him with its murderous claws ejected for the attack. I let the shot off as I blinked and tagged the cougar in the torso, just as it swiped its claws at my grandfather, slashing his forearm. The wounded cat fell to the ground and whimpered in pain. Poppa used his hunting knife to end the cat's misery with a swift swipe to the neck. Then, he walked over to me and hugged me with one arm. "Good job, Amir. I knew you had it in you."

After packing the gun, I helped Poppa stop the bleeding by tying his shirt around the gashes. The wound looked painful, but Poppa never panicked. The way Poppa remained stoic when he drove to the hospital was impressive. He didn't groan from the pain, but I never heard some of the obscenities he said that day again.

As I lay there in my hospital bed, I looked over at the scars on Poppa's forearm. The scars were a little reminder of what it took to teach me how to be a man. The sacrifices my grandparents made to raise me right can never be repaid.

Black hung around until he grew sleepy. When he left for home, he told me he would be back the next day to check on me. My grandparents decided to stay the night at the hospital. I refused, but there was no way Nana was going to leave me that night. I decided not to argue the point. Nana slept in the open bed beside me, and Poppa tried his best to make himself comfortable sleeping in the chair on the other side. For some reason, having them there made me feel safe again.

The next morning, Dr. Bryant woke us, as she entered the room with her clipboard and my file in her hand. Poppa and Nana awoke as I did when Dr. Bryant walked in.

She excused herself, "I'm sorry. I didn't know there were visitors here."

Poppa quickly stood up and introduced himself. "Oh, it's okay, Doctor. It's just about time to get up anyway. Come in. We're Amir's grandparents." Dr. Bryant proceeded into the room and put her clipboard on the table beside me.

"I'm Dr. Bryant. It's nice to see Amir has such a loving family who supports him, because he will need it."

Nana popped up and included herself into the conversation. "What do you mean? What kind of support will Amir need?"

Dr. Bryant directed a question at me. "You didn't tell them, Ace?"

I reluctantly answered, "Not yet."

Poppa butted in. "Tell us what, Ace?"

Dr. Bryant felt the need to step in and take over. "Do you want to tell them, or do you want me to tell them, Ace?"

I nodded my head, and my morning voice cracked as I said, "You do it."

Dr. Bryant opened my file and took out x-rays of my vertebrae and pinned them to the light box on the wall and started to explain. "Ace's vertebra was fractured when the bullet grazed against it. But, as you can see, there was no structural harm to the spinal canal, nor the spinal cord itself, which can only mean Ace is temporarily paralyzed due to the nerve damage the bullet caused."

Nana couldn't stop herself from interrupting Dr. Bryant. "Paralyzed?"

Poppa stepped in to let the doctor finish. "The doctor said it was temporary."

Dr. Bryant continued, "Yes, it will be temporary as long as Ace goes through physical therapy to regain mobility. The process is not easy, and it will take some time, but as long as, Ace is willing to do the work, he should be able to fully regain mobility in his legs."

Poppa breathed deeply ingesting the news and stood up. He walked over to my bedside and put a hand on my shoulder.

"Well, it looks like we got work to do, Amir. You will beat this. I know you can."

Dr. Bryant continued, "As soon as Ace heals from his wounds, we will start physical therapy."

III

Learning how to walk again was the most challenging feat I've ever had to accomplish, but the daily therapy sessions with Dr. Bryant finally started to work after a couple of weeks of frustration and doubt. No matter how much I cursed and complained, Dr. Bryant kept a positive attitude. If it were not for her encouragement, I would have never recovered. My constant agitation was stemmed from fear of the worst possible outcome, but the worries began to subside when I gained some feeling back in my toes.

The feeling of being back on my own feet was a sensation nothing compares to. The cold linoleum floor felt like heaven against my skin; it was the closest I had ever been to walking on clouds. My legs were still weak, but my progress was steady.

Dr. Bryant was surprised at how fast I was recovering. She kept telling me how the healing process has to do with the patient's mental willpower and that I had a lot of it. Determination is something that was instilled in me as a child because I had to earn everything that came to me.

Because my mom was gone, I had to grow up faster than the average kid. I had developed more respect for my grand-parents, and I loved them too much to watch them struggle to take care of me. Nana was forced to retire because of her heart, and it seemed like Poppa was making just enough to pay the bills. You could feel the somber energy around the house for days at a time.

Sometimes, Poppa would come home from work, eat and go to sleep until he had to leave again in the morning. The only time the ambiance changed in the house was on Sundays, when Poppa watched football and knocked back a dozen cold ones. Nana would be in church half of the day on Sundays, so Poppa got away with a little more mischief than usual, or so he thought. Nana was well aware of his weekly activities, but she knew that was Poppa's only time to find solace.

The summer after I finished middle school, I discovered a lot about myself and what I was capable of. Summer vacation had just begun, and June gloom was still in full effect when Black invited me to a party we were too young go to. Protesting the idea was pointless.

Black taunted me, "You're a fucking pussy, and I'll never talk to you again if you don't go. This is my big cousin's party. Everybody who is anybody around this mutha' fucka' will be there."

Peer pressure persuaded me to sneak out of the house shortly after Nana passed out on the couch that night. James and Black were creased up in grown men's clothes and

wore obviously fake jewelry with tooth-
picks in their mouths.

I had to ask, "What's with the tooth-
picks?"

James replied, "What are you wearing?"
I was underdressed in my *Ninja Turtle* t-
shirt and jeans.

Black jumped in, "I invited you to THE
party of all parties, and this is how you do
me? Fuck it! We're already late. Let's just
go."

The subway train we hopped on was
nearly empty, except for an old lady
crocheting away and a homeless man who
slept with his mouth agape, making one
side of the cabin air pungent with the stench
of malt liquor.

We sat as far away as possible from the
stench of the homeless man, and the old
lady peeked up at us over the brim of her
glasses with skinny eyes. The old lady must
have known we were up to no good; her
grandmother's intuition was keen. We
smirked and paid the old lady no mind, but

her eyes repeatedly jumped back and forth from her knitting project to us.

Black took the first shot at my outfit, "I wouldn't have invited you the party if I knew you were gonna dress like Steve Urkel's little brother, Ace. I should make you turn that shit inside out."

I was quick to comeback that time. "I didn't know this was a broke pimp theme party. You're lucky I was able to get out of the house. I can't even breathe in that place without being asked what I'm doing."

Black wasn't the least bit offended, "Shit, we look fresh. Just don't cry when you get laughed at."

James purposely cleared his throat and interrupted the bickering, then looked at me deadpan and pulled out a silver flask with gold trimming and held it back out of view of the old lady. James smiled showing all of his teeth. My eyes went big.

Black blurted out, "That's what I'm talking about. That's why you my nigga, James. Always thinking ahead."

The old lady scrunched her eyebrows to observe the sudden commotion. We ignored her gaze. James unscrewed the top of the flask and smelled the aroma of its contents and said, "This was my granddaddy's flask. He was gonna give it to me when I turned twenty-one, but he got real sick, so he gave it to me a few years early. None of my family members know I have the flask, and I'd like to keep it that way."

James knocked back a big gulp and scrunched his face, feeling the burn. James passed the flask to Black. After he took a swig, he belched and made a refreshing sound. Black complimented James' grandfather's taste. "Your granddaddy drank some good shit, James. We're 'bout to be fucked up!" I was next in the relay. As Black passed the flask to me, my stomach suddenly filled with butterflies.

The only alcohol I had ever drunk was the wine shots that I stole from the communion tray at church one Sunday. Mom tore my ass up when we got home, and I threw up all over everything at the dinner table.

The strong smell of alcohol made my pubescent nose hairs curl up inside my nostrils as I peered into the flask and observed the dark liquid; then, I swished it around. James got tired of waiting.

"Stop playing around and drink some before I take my shit back. It might put some hair on your bird chest and hopefully melt that Ninja Turtle design off your shirt."

Black laughed too hard and provoked me to swallow more liquor than intended when I took the shot. The alcohol set my chest on fire as it passed my tonsils. James and Black pounded fists while laughing with and at me. Then, James grabbed the flask just as the old lady looked up to see the transaction.

The old lady snatched off her glasses and threw a small fit when she saw the flask. "Y'all know y'all are acting up. Where are your parents? You should be ashamed of yourselves. Your mothers would be ashamed of you I'm sure."

The old lady must have struck a nerve as the alcohol kicked in because I couldn't stop myself from disrespecting her. "You don't know anything about my mother you old bitch. Why don't you mind your own business?"

The old lady shook her head and preached, "Lord, these kids need Jesus." James and Black looked at me with their mouths open, shocked and snickering.

Amused by my disrespect for elders, Black said, "That must have been the alcohol talking. Give him some more. I like drunk Ace." James chuckled at Black's comment, but even though I felt the buzz, the drink is not what caused me to snap at the old lady.

The liquor in the flask didn't make it to the party. By the time we arrived to Black's cousin's house on the West side of the city, the liquor was gone. The middle-class community was mostly an African American suburban neighborhood. The homes were cookie-cutter, and every lawn was meticulously manicured and evenly green in every corner. Our stroll changed a bit with liquor in our system as we approached Black's cousin's house and rang the doorbell.

The bass from the speakers vibrated the house with gangster rap music, until the door opened revealing a scantily clad woman who left all of us speechless as she stood there waiting for some kind of reaction. The scantily clad woman took a sip from her straw and raised an eyebrow at the sight of us and said, "Okay, let me guess, two broke pimps and a nerd. But I don't get it. It's not Halloween, and we ain't got no candy. So, what ya'll want?"

Black was the only one who had the right to answer her question. "We ain't here for no damn candy. We're here for the party."

The scantily clad woman laughed in confusion. "This party is a grown folks party, no minors, and no Ninja Turtle t-shirts. Bye!" Black and James looked at me as the door slammed in our faces.

Black was embarrassed. "I knew I should have left your 'turtle power' ass at home."

Black annoyingly rang the doorbell again until the door swung open. This time a man wearing a black leather outfit with designer shades and too much jewelry answered the door. The shiny man lifted up his shades to look at Black and shouted, "Cuzzo, you made it." Black's cousin drunkenly hugged Black and routinely roughed him up a bit.

Then, he looked at us and said, "You didn't tell me you were bringing the Goof Troop. Do your parents know where you are?"

We all shook our heads "no." Black's cousin laughed, "Good. I'm Nuke. It's my birthday, and this is my house. I'm gonna let you lil' niggas come in, but you better not fuck shit up. Remember three things and you'll be good: don't touch my bitch, don't touch my weed, and don't touch my money." Nuke pointed at me, "And you, you gotta change your shirt. You can't come in like that. You're making me look bad."

The house was full of intoxicated people who stared us down as we walked through the party following Nuke. As we passed the scantily clad woman, she smirked and said, "My bad. I didn't know you were babysitting tonight, Nuke!"

Some of the party people laughed, but Nuke ignored them and said, "Don't worry about that. Ya'll good. I was doing the same thing when I was your age, but look at me now. Some of us just grow up a little faster than others. Whatever you do in this world, you gotta respect yourself enough to not let people walk all over you. It's not what you do but how you do it."

After changing my wardrobe, I got back to the party to find James and Black, but I could hardly see through the dark smoke-filled room. The dance floor was flooded with grinding bodies as the disco lights briefly gave everyone the spotlight.

The crowd was thick as I pushed my way to the other side of the room. I spotted James trying to dance with a woman whose breasts were bigger than his head. The busty woman was amused by James' attempt and let him grind on her from behind, until she twerked on him so hard, he fell back into the wall.

The busty woman laughed, and so did I. Nuke walked over and helped James get to his feet and said, "Why you do this youngin' like that? You know he can't handle all that ass." The busty woman shrugged and continued to party. James was humiliated by his inability to perform on the dance floor, so he walked out the house into the backyard. I followed behind to anta-gonize him while the wound was still fresh, because that's what best friends do.

When I walked out of the backdoor, James was nowhere to be found in a small crowd of conversing people. Black was sitting at a table with three men playing dominoes when he saw me exit the back door and waved me over.

The men at the table were dressed in designer clothes and were well groomed; one of them wore a red suit, one of them wore a top hat and suspenders, and the other wore a black fitted V-neck. Their jewelry was not as offensive as Nuke's but still had the capability to blind a man. A robust blunt was passed around while they sipped expensive cognac on the rocks, and a small stack of hundred dollar bills was folded on the table.

Black introduced me as I walked up, "This is my lil' homie, Ace." The men looked at me and nodded without saying a word. The man in the V-neck tried to pass me the blunt, but I declined the offer. Black looked at me like a disappointed older brother, as one of the men gave me orders.

"You better hit that shit. Can't be kicking it with the big homies if you ain't with the program." The men chuckled and continued to play without looking up. I wasn't about to look like a chump.

I snatched the blunt from Black and took a long drag like a pro, but I was quickly renounced to amateur when I nearly fell to my knees, coughing up my lungs. The man under the top hat tried to help. He told me to put my arms behind my head; then, he passed me some cognac in a cup. The watered-down alcohol soothed my throat and warmed my belly. My eyes were bloodshot and watery, and I could feel an instant head change as I started to giggle for no reason.

Black's teammate slammed a domino on the table; then, he took off his hat and yelled, "That's twenty, and that's game." Black's teammate snapped his suspenders obnoxiously, grabbed the money off the table and gave a cut to Black.

The other team argued about the loss as the man in the red suit said, "Come on. Let's run it back. Double or nothing, but I need a new partner. This fool is giving up points." He was as hot as his suit when he asked me, "You know how to play, youngsta?" I nodded my head "yes."

My grandfather and I played dominos all the time. He taught me everything he knows about the game. The red-suited man was ready for revenge, "Ok, let's see what you got."

Domino after domino that I slammed on the table added points on the board. My teammate smiled in amazement at my skill level. Black's bewildered expression was priceless. He watched me score with almost every domino I laid on the table. I never knew how well Poppa taught me because he never let me win. He always said, "The more I challenge you, the better you will become. I will never let you win because neither would anyone else. You either earn your victory or learn from your defeat." My first victory made me feel like the heavyweight champion of the world as I slammed the domino on the table for the win.

Black couldn't believe what just happened, as he stayed silent trying to grasp reality. After my teammate got his money back, he split the stack then handed half to me and said, "I just broke even, but you earned this lil' homie. You got game. You go by Ace, right?"

I replied with pride. "That's what they call me."

The red-suited man offered a handshake while saying, "They call me JayBird…."

Before JayBird could finish his sentence, a shadowy figure in the distance popped over the backyard's brick wall wearing all black and a ski mask. After getting a better look at the figure, I could see him wielding a double-barrel sawed-off shotgun, as he aimed in our directions. No one else seemed to be aware of the gunman as the dark figure raised his weapon to fire a shot.

My heart sank as I managed to yell, "Watch out!" I clutched JayBird's extended hand and pulled Black to the ground and out of harm's way before the gunman pulled the trigger. Black's teammate also tried to jump out of the way leaving his top hat on the table as his legs got riddled with pellets. Shells were released as the gunman cocked the shotgun and prepared to let off another round when the man in the black V-neck pulled out a shiny Desert Eagle from the small of his back.

Party people scattered as the gunman shot again, destroying the domino table and top hat just as the Desert Eagle banged a few rounds at the assailant. The bullets re-sculpted the architecture, as the gunman quickly disappeared behind the newly designed brick wall.

JayBird stood up and ran over to Black's teammate and kneeled over him as he lay there squirming in pain from the pellets that entered his thigh. JayBird tried not to panic as he checked the wounds, only to find that his leg was merely grazed by a pellet. The anxiety in my stomach made me nauseous as Black lifted me back on my feet and asked, "You good, Ace?" I was on my feet momentarily, but my legs collapsed under me, and I fell to my knees.

Nuke rushed out of the house after the commotion and saw Black picking me up from the ground again. Nuke helped Black stand me up; then, he quickly explained,

"We have to get y'all out of here before the cops show up. You don't need to be in the mix when they get here."

JayBird overheard Nuke and volunteered to give us a ride home, as he expressed, "It's the least I can do."

James finally emerged from the house walking and talking sideways, as he managed to slur, "What happened?" before falling flat on his face into the grass.

We rolled James over and picked him up as he blurted out, "I told you. I'm legal. Don't let the baby face fool you."

The tires on JayBird's SUV screeched as we sped out of the suburban neighborhood and back to the city. The ride home was quiet as we tried to digest what just took place at the party. James slept against the rear seat window, snoring the alcohol out of his system. Black sat in the front passenger seat, and I sat behind him.

JayBird finally took the opportunity to speak to us. "I'm sorry you youngstas got caught up in the right place at the wrong time tonight. I just want you to know we're not the bad guys. Some people just can't stand to see brothas like us come up from nothing. One thing you have to remember is success can turn allies into enemies. Only the people who were there from day one eat when the table is full, but if they get greedy, you cut them off before they sink the ship." JayBird's explanation relieved my mind, and I felt my whole body settle from the tension.

Black was dropped off at his house first, and he carried an unconscious James over his shoulder. I started to get out of the SUV too when JayBird told me he would take me home even though my house was in walking distance from Black's.

When we approached my grandparents' house, JayBird pulled over and parked. He turned the lights off as he said, "Hold on a minute, Ace. I wanna talk to you."

I watched JayBird pull out a fat bankroll from his pocket and unexpectedly tossed it into my lap and said, "That right there is for you, Ace. For saving my life tonight."

My face lit up as I expressed my gratitude. "Wow! For real?"

JayBird reassured me, "Yup, that's just a small thank you. I would have been dead if it were not for you. You got a lot of heart for a young cat, Ace. You remind me of myself when I was your age."

The top bill became saturated from the sweat on my hands. I still couldn't believe the money was mine as I said, "You have no idea how much my family needs this right now. Thank you!"

JayBird was stuck in the moment and thought hard before he replied. "Just a small token of my appreciation, Ace. You're a stand up young man. If you're ever looking to make some extra cash let me know. There's always room on the team for somebody like you."

JayBird slipped a business card to me and said, "Don't hesitate to call if you need something, Ace. Think of me as a big brother, okay?" I nodded in agreement, having new family was the opposite of what I was used to. That was the first time I felt a genuine positive vibe since Mom had been gone. I reached over and pounded JayBird's fist before I started for the house.

Sleep never found me that night, and I tried my hardest to stay calm in my room as I counted the bankroll JayBird gave to me. I had never seen so much money in real life, and I was afraid that if I fell asleep I would wake up and realize it was just a dream.

After spreading the money out on my bed, I counted ten thousand dollars seven times to make sure. Then, I stashed half of the money in one of my faded pairs of Chuck Taylors. The other half was going to Nana and Poppa, so I sealed it in a blank envelope. The daylight slowly took away the night as I lay in bed daydreaming about what I was going to do with the money.

The mailman usually showed up early in the day, so I did a mini stakeout by the window, so I could intercept the mail before Nana. Nana was in the kitchen making breakfast for the both of us when I spotted the mailman and broke into action. I met the mailman at the box, and he handed over the mail to me and wished me a good day.

Before I walked back inside the house, I slid the money envelope into the middle of the stack; then, I put the stack on the dining room table when I got back inside. The anxiety was killing me as I informed Nana, "The mail just came." Nana paid little attention to me. She nodded and continued making breakfast.

After eating breakfast, I cleared the table and started washing the dishes, hopeful that it would make Nana check the mail. Nana took the bait and started going through what she thought was nothing but bills. I kept looking back at her from the sink with excitement as she said without looking up, "You never looked so happy to be washing dishes, Amir. Wish you would do that more often, sugar. I'd appreciate the help."

When Nana finally got to the envelope, she became skeptical. "Who sent this? How can you send a letter with no stamp or return address?" Nana shook the envelope to guess its contents.

I played along and said, "Open it, Nana. The mailman gave it to me. Maybe whatever is inside will tell you whom it belongs to." Nana reluctantly started to open the envelope. The task seemed to be a decade long as I waited impatiently for her reaction.

Nana opened the envelope and removed a folded sheet of letter paper and discovered the cash. She shouted in disbelief, "Oh, my God. Is this real?" After picking up the money, the letter revealed a handwritten message that read:

"Your family deserves this more than anyone I know. Please accept this gift as a token of appreciation."

Tears began flowing from Nana's eyes. As I embraced her with a hug, she gave praise. "Thank the Lord, baby! Thank the Lord! We gone be alright, Amir. Baby, He's watching over us." Nana hugged me tightly, and although helping my family felt good, I knew the money would run out eventually, and we would be right back where we started.

Poppa came home early that night, and the three of us went out for a steak dinner to celebrate. Nana needed a break from the kitchen, and Poppa had to stay awake after dinner and interact with us. After we ate, we stayed at the restaurant talking until it was time to close.

I tried to sleep that night, but everything JayBird said to me played back in my head like a song on repeat and kept me awake for hours. Helping my grandparents and putting money on my mom's books was my main concern, and JayBird treated me like family, so I knew I could count on his word. Since insomnia got the better of me, I decided to call JayBird at an inappropriate hour. Luckily, he answered and told me to meet him at his warehouse the next morning.

The next day, I woke up early and told Nana I was going to play ball with James and Black. Nana wouldn't have let me work, especially at a warehouse. I had to figure out a way that could happen on a daily basis without her knowing.

JayBird's warehouse bustled with activity as employees hustled on the clock. A variety of products were stacked high, getting shipped in and out of the warehouse. The security guard at the entrance directed me upstairs to JayBird's office, which overlooked the entire warehouse. JayBird was arguing on the phone when I arrived at his office. He motioned for me to sit down while he finished the conversation. JayBird was furious as he barked orders through the phone.

"I don't care if it takes all day. I know that package was on your truck. If it doesn't show up, it's coming out of your paycheck." JayBird slammed the phone back on the receiver and apologized for the improper introduction.

JayBird gave me a tour of the warehouse while introducing me to all of his employees like I was some type of celebrity, telling them I was his "little brother from another mother."

After showing me around the warehouse, we went back to JayBird's office and sat down. JayBird proceeded to give me the rundown. "Tomorrow, we start training. You will learn every job, but initially you're going to work under me, as my assistant. I want you to be the eyes behind my head. You're good at that."

IV

Supporting my own body weight required every ounce of strength I possessed. Even walking a few feet every day felt like running a marathon, but the support from my grandparents and friends gave me strength when I had none left. Every time James came to visit, he came at me with a joke. Once, he popped his head into my room from the hallway and said, "Bruh, is it true? The nurse just said you were breakdancing in the hallway for tips last night."

James and Black helped me to keep a sense of humor throughout my rehabilitation. Sometimes, Dr. Bryant asked them to leave the room during our therapy sessions because I couldn't focus. There I was trying to walk from one side of the room to the other when Black said, "Just imagine a big ol' booty in front of you. You gotta get the booty, Ace." Black's comment nearly made me fall, but Dr. Bryant helped me find my balance and asked Black to leave the room immediately. Dr. Bryant treated us like disobedient grade-schoolers when we got out of control, but she knew the laughter would only help me heal in the long run.

Thinking about my kids also gave me strength even though the last time I saw them was at a custody hearing. Keeping a positive environment during the healing process was something Dr. Bryant was adamant about, and contacting Joy would only disturb the peace.

Having a normal conversation with Joy was impossible because she never wanted to hear what I had to say, and I couldn't blame her considering the heartache I put her through. Admitting that my actions changed Joy's attitude towards me was not hard, but accepting the fact that I could no longer get back what I had with her was. Only time would tell if Joy could ever treat me like a normal human being one day for the sake of our children's upbringing.

Joy and I met as freshmen in high school. She was the new girl from out of state and often the topic of discussion amongst the homies when we talked about girls. The hate was strong when my boys found out that Joy and I had four classes together. Little did they know she never looked my way, and every time I tried to talk to her, she cut the conversation short.

It wasn't until I saw Joy alone after school one day crying in the bleachers on the football field did she actually hold a conversation with me. Joy was startled when she took her hands from her face and saw me walking up the bleachers. She tried to dry her tears with her sleeves and act normal. As I approached Joy, her voice was shaky when she asked, "What does a girl have to do to be alone around here?"

I answered, "Well, you could drop kick me, and I'll go flying down these bleachers. I might break my neck or leg or something, but at least you will be alone again." Joy cracked a smile and shook her head at my ridiculousness. I seized the moment and said, "Uh oh, was that a smile? Don't try to act like it wasn't. I'll take my joke back if I have to." Joy laughed, amused at my attempt to cheer her up.

She said, "You're kinda funny when you're not trying to spit that weak ass game like you do in class." The fact that Joy said a sentence longer than two words to me was a plus, and even though she had dissed my game, I was making progress.

I sat next to Joy on the bleachers and tried to get her to open up, "You wanna talk about it?" Joy hesitated before answering.

Then, reluctantly she said, "My ex-boyfriend from back home is with what used to be my best friend. He knew I was moving, and he said we'd make it work. It's only been three weeks. He didn't even try. Last night, he said a long distance relationship is too hard, but he still had feelings for me. I don't see how that is if he's with my best friend. Neither of them had the guts to tell me, but they posted a picture of themselves all hugged up online."

A tear rolled down Joy's cheek, and I wiped it away with my thumb as she asked me, "How can two people who claim they love me hurt me so bad?" I wasn't expecting to be bombarded with that type of information all at once, but I tried my best to say the right words.

"I honestly don't know, but they say everything happens for a reason. People like that don't deserve a place in your life. They deserve each other. But you, you deserve better friends. You know, like me."

Joy chuckled and said, "Oh really? What makes you so much better?"

I thought of the one thing that would cheer up anyone, and I answered, "The fact that I'm about to buy you ice cream makes me better."

Joy smiled and nodded her head in agreement. "It's a start," she said.

Joy and I got together a few weeks after the talk on the bleachers, and about a year later, Joy got pregnant with Junior. We both dropped out of high school as sophomores. Joy's parents were furious. They tried their hardest to convince her not to have the baby, but she went against their commands even though the ultimatum was getting kicked out of the house. Nana and Poppa were both disappointed in me, but overall they were happy about the new addition to the family.

Joy moved into my grandparent's house halfway through the pregnancy. By that time, I had been working with JayBird for over a year. JayBird took me under his wing and taught me how to run the business. I was his right-hand man and made more money than I needed at fifteen years old. A lot of the money went to the house. I told my grandparents I had an after-school job on campus, so they never questioned me. They were thankful for the help more than anything.

With a newborn on the way, I needed to make more money. So, I told JayBird about my situation hoping he could help me make ends meet. JayBird didn't want me to drop out of school, but I had to provide for my new family. So, he reluctantly agreed to give me a promotion.

JayBird asked me to come to the warehouse late one night. I didn't know what to expect because I knew no one else would be there. The warehouse was dark except for the lights from JayBird's office that shined brightly enough for me to see the pathway through the aisles. Before I reached JayBird's office, he heard my footsteps approaching and invited me in.

"Ace, glad you could make it. Come on in and have a seat." JayBird finished up with some busy work on his laptop as I made myself comfortable.

The mouse clicked a few more times before JayBird diverted his attention towards me and said, "So you're ready to move up to the big leagues. Is that right

Ace?" I felt like I entered the draft to go pro.

My game face was on as I replied, "Put me in coach. I was born ready." JayBird was amused at my eagerness.

He wanted to find out how ready I was and said, "We'll see about that. This is serious business, but I know you can handle it. You're going to see some things that you can't unsee. This job is not for the weak or the scared, so let me know now if you're not up for the challenge. I trust you more than any of my other employees, but I need your word that what happens here, stays here."

No way could I ever snitch on JayBird after everything he had done for me, but I reassured him anyway. "You're like family to me, and I would never betray family."

JayBird could sense my sincerity, as he looked me directly in my eyes and said, "I know, and that's why you're my shadow, because you're a man of your word." No one ever referred to me as a man. I rubbed my chin to groom my barely existent facial hair. JayBird stood and motioned for me to follow him.

JayBird led me towards the back of the warehouse to a janitor's closet, and he opened the door and clicked the light on. Cleaning supplies occupied the cramped janitor's closet. I stared at the supplies confusedly as JayBird said, "What? You said you wanted to make more money right?"

I grabbed a mop from inside of the closet and questioned JayBird. "This is what you call a promotion?" JayBird laughed and walked into the closet with me closing the door behind him.

He pulled out a TV remote from his pocket and said, "You should have seen the look on your face."

JayBird punched in four numbers on the remote. I flinched when pressure released from hydraulic pumps and the far wall that held cleaning supplies on mounted shelves started to move. The wall spun one hundred eighty degrees to reveal a narrow pathway. The trick door revolved back to its original position as we walked a short distance down the cemented hallway.

At the end of the hallway, steel hatch doors were hinged to the ground. A surveillance camera watched us as JayBird knocked on the metal doors with his foot. The door clanked loudly as it was unlocked from the other side and pushed open to reveal stairs. A monster of a man was on the other side of the door holding guard. A firearm was tucked away in his shoulder holster. JayBird greeted the guard with a simple head nod as we walked down the stairs into the hidden underground level.

Nothing could prepare me for what I was about to encounter as I laid my eyes on the biggest drug operation I had ever seen in real life. The sight was like something out of a movie, as employees in safety gear continued to do work without acknowledging our presence.

There were four stations throughout the room that carried out different tasks like an assembly line. One table weighed and separated the products, which would be taken to the next table to be properly packaged. After being packaged, the next table put the narcotics in disguise, concealing them in cheap ceramic artwork. The final table put the ceramics into shipping boxes and made sure they were tagged with the addresses that matched the order forms. The boxes stayed underground until they were taken to the main warehouse just before the regular employees came into work to start shipping packages.

JayBird saw me standing there looking uncomfortable and proceeded to say, "You don't have to do this if you don't want to, Ace. This life ain't for everybody. Like I said before, it's not for the weak or scared, but understand that scared money don't make money. I would never encourage you to do something that you're not comfortable with. The choice is yours." I was actually more excited other than anything, but my skittish energy made me look out of place.

There was not a chance that I would pass up that type of opportunity even though I was aware of the risks I was about take. My son would be born soon, and there weren't a lot of jobs out there for fifteen year olds, and working part time wasn't going to feed my family. The only fear that I was experiencing at the moment was the possibility of failing my unborn son and Joy, and that terrified me. No way would I ever be anything like my father. I made a promise to myself that I would do everything in my power to provide my family with the life they deserved.

JayBird took me around to each station and introduced me to everyone, while they explained what they did. The process was fascinating as I observed the well-oiled machine in motion. JayBird told me that he didn't want me handling any of the drugs. I would be more of an extra set of eyes to make sure all the products were accounted for and ready to be shipped to the right addresses in the morning.

The operation had been running into some internal issues recently. JayBird pulled me to the side and explained the situation in a low voice that only I could hear. "I don't know who it is yet, but somebody down here is fucking up or somebody is stealing from the cookie jar. You're going to be my quality control, Ace. I know how you are, and you don't let anything get past you. If anybody down here gives you any shit, let me know so we can take care of it on sight."

I was overwhelmed having so much responsibility in an environment that I was unfamiliar with, but I was used to being thrown to the wolves and holding my own. Plus, I wasn't going to let JayBird down after he had done so much for my grand-parents and me.

As my son grew inside of Joy, leaving every night for the warehouse became difficult. I constantly worried about how Joy was dealing with being exiled from her family during a time when she needed them the most. Joy's mother reached out to us several times, but her father pushed her out of the house and his life. When she left home, it was against her mother's wishes, but the environment was not healthy for a child to develop in the womb.

Joy was safe with my grandparents, but I still worried with her being so close to her due date. Joy's sister spent the night with her sometimes while I worked. It gave them time to catch up with each other, and Joy didn't have to bother my grandparents if she needed assistance. Joy didn't like to inconvenience them, but my grandparents were happy to have her there. Nana had nothing but time on her hands. Having Joy around made my grandparent's house feel like a home again. As we all anticipated the arrival of our newest family member, it pulled us closer together.

The money that I was making at the warehouse was triple my previous pay, but I kept that to myself because the family thought I worked with the local newspaper making deliveries before dawn. The type of deliveries I was involved with was a little different, but they didn't need to know that.

The orders were getting bigger every night as new clientele was added to the order forms daily, which meant I had to pay close attention to the packages that were incoming and outgoing. With so much going on at one time, making an error was easy to do, so I tried to double and triple check before approving anything. I tried my best to focus but was constantly distracted due to the fact that Joy could go into labor at any time. I checked my cell phone every two minutes to ensure I didn't miss a call or text. The warehouse was loud when employees hustled to meet the morning deadlines, and I probably wouldn't hear it ringing.

The most hectic night since I started working the graveyard shift was well underway when I got the call. Joy's water had broken, and she went into labor. I told Poppa I would meet them at the hospital, as I left work feeling anxious to meet my son for the first time. I was almost out of the steel hatch doors when I realized my backpack was left behind, so I went back for it. When I walked back to get my bag, I noticed one of the employees placing a shipping label on top of a label that was already on the box. I didn't make anything of it as I dashed for the hospital.

Joy arrived just a few minutes before me, and she was getting helped into bed as I entered the labor ward. Nana and Poppa waited in the lobby for us to get situated. I waited for the nurses to finish hooking Joy up to all of the machines before walking to her bedside to hold her hand. I kissed Joy on the forehead and said, "I can't believe I'm about to witness a miracle. You're a gift from God and so is our son. I'm lucky to have you both in my life." I saw Joy's eyes get moist, and she couldn't control the tears from escaping.

When I went to the lobby to tell my grandparents to come to the room, Joy's mom and sister surprised me as they engaged in conversation with Nana and Poppa. Joy was in labor for four hours before she was dilated enough to have the baby. She had a natural birth even though the doctors recommended the epidural when she cried out from the pressure of the contractions. Joy is a strong woman, and she knew what her body was capable of, and I was there to support her in any way possible.

When I held my son for the first time, I had an out of body experience. Nothing other than us existed in the universe at that moment. I looked at Joy admiring her strength as she lay there drenched in sweat, exhausted from the last nine months of doing nature's work.

We all stood around the bed and looked at Joy hold our son for the first time. Suddenly, a knock on the slightly open door caught our attention. I answered the knock and told the person to enter, assuming it was hospital staff. We were all stunned when Joy's father walked into the room. No one said a word to him even though he greeted us with a simple, "Hey y'all."

We must have all been feeling the same way because nobody spoke back, and everyone avoided eye contact. Joy's dad knew he was in the wrong, so he started talking before somebody said something to him first.

"Look, I know nobody wants to see me right now, but I had to come apologize to my daughter and grandson. There's no excuse for how I reacted to the situation, but I will say that I acted out of anger. That is not an excuse for letting my anger get the best of me, and I wish I would have realized that I was acting like a damn fool. I know there's nothing I can do to make it up to you, but if you can find it in your heart to forgive a foolish old man, I'll try my best to restore our family and help you with anything that you need."

The apology from Joy's dad threw us off because we all resented him for how he treated his own flesh and blood, and even though his apology was sincere, I still had negative feelings towards him. After an extended awkward silence, Joy's father mumbled, "Well, I tried. Love you, baby girl." Then, he turned to exit the room.

Joy let her father walk out of the room. Then, she tried to call after him but was still too weak, and her voice was barely audible. I went into the hallway and asked Joy's dad to come back in the room. When we returned, Joy responded to her dad, "I accept your apology, but I'm not moving back home. I still can't get over the fact that you pushed me away, but I'll try my best to forgive you."

That was better than nothing, and Joy had the right to feel the way she did at the time. When Joy's father held his grandson for the first time, he cried like a baby. We still don't know if they were tears of joy or tears of guilt, but they were definitely real.

We took Junior home the next day, and he was a surprisingly calm baby who slept most of the day. Junior only cried when he was hungry or needed to be changed. He was a chill baby, and that was a big plus.

I still wasn't old enough to smoke, but Poppa bought a cigar for me anyway. The taste took a little getting used to, but I eventually stopped coughing after every drag as we puffed away in the garage. Poppa gave me a tip: "You're not supposed to inhale. Just puff and release."

Poppa showed off some pieces from his gun collection and even let me hold a few. I don't know if it was the beer or the baby that was causing that weird behavior, but I was shocked when he told me, "All of these are going to be yours one day. You might as well get familiar with them." I looked at him like he wasn't speaking English, and he confirmed his statement, "Yea that's what I said. I can't take them to the grave with me, and I don't know another man who is as worthy." Poppa finally gave me his blessing after all that we went through.

Joy rested, and I put Junior to bed that night. She looked so peaceful lying there. I watched her sleep and wondered what she was dreaming about. I had never thought I would be that young with a family of my own, but the feeling was serene.

Just as I lay down beside Joy, JayBird called my cell. I answered the phone, and he said, "Congratulations, boy! I heard you had that baby last night. I just got your message about leaving for the hospital. We had a little situation that night. I know you're on baby duty for a couple of weeks, but I need to talk to you in person. The sooner the better." I told JayBird that I would be in his office first thing in the morning and thanked him for his well wishes.

When I tried to leave the next morning, Joy fussed and said, "Junior just came home last night, and they're already bugging you. Why can't they tell you what you need to know over the phone? I don't get it."

The information she asked about was off limits, so I gave her an answer that led nowhere: "Your guess is as good as mine. I promise I'll be in and out and back before you notice that I left."

Joy didn't like the answer, but it was the only one I had. She stopped her rant and said, "Straight there and straight back, or else..." I took the warning seriously, and I kissed her cheek. Then, I kissed my baby boy on his forehead before leaving.

The warehouse was full of regular employees that I had not seen in months. Some of them gave me a warm welcome and picked me up against my will and threw me into a bin of flattened boxes and said, "Congrats, big daddy." I tried to be mad but laughter got the best of me. I missed playing pranks with co-workers, and if I remember correctly, a few of them said they owed me some payback. I guess that made us even.

JayBird was usually busy with something when I came into his office, but that day he just sat there as if something was really bothering him, until he saw me approaching and changed his demeanor. He tried hard to put a mask on as I came in.

When I entered, he said, "There he his. The man himself, the only mature person in this building besides me." JayBird laughed at his own joke and stood up to greet me with a handshake hug. "I won't keep you long. I know you got that baby at home, so you need to get back."

I agreed and said, "You're lucky I even showed up. Joy was on my ass like boxer briefs. I probably can't even sit on the front porch until she feels comfortable enough to be alone with the baby."

Never had I seen JayBird's office door closed. So when he closed the door before we sat down, I knew the matter was serious. JayBird got straight to point like he always did.

"The night you left to go to the hospital, one of the packages was somehow lost after it was already boxed up and scanned into the warehouse system. But the box was never scanned again, which means it never made it on a delivery truck, nor was it ever delivered to the customer. I'm not accusing you, but it's just crazy how this happened the one day you had to leave early. I questioned everybody from the night shift, and for some reason they keep pointing the finger at you, saying they saw you leave and come back to get your bag. I'm going to tell you right now. I don't believe any of them because I know you wouldn't do something like that."

For a second I thought he was going to place the blame on me, but I'm glad he trusted me enough to doubt the rumors. I reinforced his statement by saying, "Come on, they really tried to play me like that? I wouldn't have shit right now if I never met you."

JayBird replied, "And I would probably be dead if I never met you. Don't worry about it. They're jealous. You're half their age, and you have to babysit a group of untrustworthy adults." Our bond was stronger than a business relationship.

JayBird was trying to investigate as he asked me, "Do you remember seeing any-thing unusual that night? Anything at all?"

All I could think of lately was my baby boy and Joy, so it was possible for something to slip by me without noticing, but I told him, "I remember one of the guys putting a new shipping label on top of the one that was already in place. I thought they might have just made an error on the first label, so I let it go."

The information made JayBird both relieved and furious, so he inquired about culprit. "Do you remember who made the switch?" There were only two guys who added shipping labels to the boxes. One of them went by Fast Lane, and he was undoubtedly the person who made the switch.

Knuckles cracked loudly as JayBird accepted the information he just learned, plotting on how he was going to handle Fast Lane. JayBird took a moment to thank me for my help. "Typical, Ace. I knew they couldn't get shit by you. That's why I wanted you there, to find out who's not loyal to the team." The praise I got from JayBird helped me build the confidence that I lacked due to the constant scorning of my character because I was a defiant adolescent.

JayBird thanked me again by reaching into his desk drawer and pulling out a bankroll. He tossed the money to me and said, "That's three weeks pay. Go home, and spend some time with your family. I'll see your grown ass in a few weeks."

V

The day I checked out of the hospital, Dr. Bryant threw me a going-away party. All of the staff from the rehabilitation ward attended. We ate slices of pound cake and drank punch out of red plastic cups. The party wasn't glamorous, but they still made me feel special nonetheless. I was walking on my own then, and even though I was using a cane, more than half of my strength had returned.

The rest of my recovery could continue without me being in the hospital. Poppa and Nana would come check on me often to see if I needed anything while I was in the hospital and after I returned home.

I went back home for the first time in six months. When I arrived home, I found my place had been broken into. The shattered glass spread across the carpet near the balcony door identified the thieves' point of entry. Black and James were with me, and they checked the rest of the house to make sure it was safe. Funny thing is, we didn't find anything missing like a normal home invasion. My jewelry was still in the nightstand next to the bed, and none of the electronics were missing. The cash was in a safe on the wall behind a painting of Mama Africa, so I know they didn't get to that.

Nana and Poppa had checked on my place every couple of days to get the mail and feed my African Grey parrots, so the break in was something that happened right before I was released from the hospital. Someone was trying to send me a message, and I received it loud and clear.

My home was invaded and my safety was in jeopardy. There was no way in hell I was going to stay there another night. Somebody was out for my head, and I needed a quiet place to lay low until I could figure out who was trying to get to me and why.

The detectives who investigated my case visited the hospital a few times during my recovery, but I had no information for them. Most of the time, I would try to keep it short with the detectives and act like I was in pain to encourage them to leave. I'm pretty sure they didn't want to be there anyway. When they asked me questions, it seemed as if they were trying to insinuate that I must have done something to deserve getting lit up like a Christmas tree. They really didn't want to solve the case. They just wanted find out *why* I got shot, and not to find the people who were responsible.

After about a year of working the graveyard shift at the warehouse, I was making enough money to move out of my grandparents' house and into a condo in the outskirts of the city. Even though living with my grandparents was an experience that brought our family closer together, the

10'x10' bedroom that I spent most of my childhood in wasn't enough space for us anymore. Jr. needed his own room, and Joy and I needed our space.

I was only seventeen at the time, but the manager of the complex doctored up the paperwork after I gave him six months of rent up front and a generous tip for his troubles.

I had kept the condo after Joy and I split up, and I decided to put a down payment on a house in the city. Only my trues knew I had that condo, so I could lay low there while I finished recovering. Black and James helped me pack some of my belongings into two suitcases; clothes and cash is all I needed to get by until things made sense again.

The first night at the condo was sleepless; my pistol laid on the pillow beside me, keeping me company even though Black and James stayed the night in case anything popped off. The last time I slept in that bed, Joy was lying beside me. I ran my hand across the mattress and felt the void of her bare soft skin against mine. Those were the days that I would do any and everything to protect and provide for my family. I was beginning to make a name for myself by hustling with JayBird, but I had to branch out and do my own thing.

I was starting to find my own clients and the only way I could move my own products was if I became one of JayBird's clients myself. JayBird was against any of his employees doing their own thing, but he was also against anyone bringing in new clients. That was his job, and no one else was involved in that process. But JayBird also knew I was too much like him, so nothing he said would have changed my mind. He had to watch me leave the nest and learn how to fly on my own.

James and Black were the only ones who knew I was hustling with JayBird outside of those I worked with in the warehouse. When I started moving weight on my own, I offered Black and James a spot on the team. They were the only ones I could trust to have my back in any shady situation that we might run into. If I were going to build an empire, I wanted it to be with my boys, my brothers. Black was on the team as soon as I proposed the idea to him. He said, "You know I'm in. Let's get this money, Ace."

James thought I was bullshitting until I received a package at my condo in the mail one day from JayBird's warehouse and broke the ceramic artwork into pieces with a hammer, releasing the concealed product from its hiding place. James went from sitting on the couch to a soldier at attention when he saw the drugs fall on the coffee table.

"Oh shit, Ace! You da' fucken man bruh. You da' fucken man!" yelled James. He rubbed his palms together to cease the itch from the money he was about to make.

One of the most important things I learned from JayBird was to never bring your work home when you're involved in the type of business that attracts unwanted attention, so we had all of our packages sent to a P. O. Box.

There was no way I could put Joy and Jr. in the middle of what I was doing to make money, and Joy still didn't know what I was up to, but she was beginning to have an idea that I was hiding something. Joy constantly accused me of cheating because I was out chasing money with my boys.

We used a fake ID to rent a storage space for us to operate out of and keep our artillery, and we bought a beat-up two-door pickup truck and some gardening supplies to throw the cops off if they were on our trail. Being flashy and flossing for the hood was the last of my concerns. The spotlight isn't exactly what you want in that line of work. One of the most important things JayBird taught me was to respect myself and respect the streets.

He preached, "Some of these cats egos grow with their money. Don't ever think you're untouchable, Ace. Humble yourself, and you will go far in life. That's how you earn the respect of the streets, while keeping your self-respect."

JayBird's truck drivers were delivering packages to us almost daily after a few months of running our own operation. James and Black were runners, making more money than they could ever imagine at their age, and so was I, but we kept a low profile. The focus was to build our client list, so we had to do our homework and put our ear to the street.

At the time, our best clients were a couple of white boys from the valley, pre-med students at the local state university who started filling prescriptions long before earning their doctorates. They were also my favorite clients because they were the most unsuspecting. Questioning them about why they always had their shirts tucked in, we had a few laughs every time we met for coffee and an exchange at the college cafeteria. James was considering taking a few classes since he was constantly at school.

Every time we met with the white boys, they were buying more and more, doubling up on almost every product we offered.

They must have been supplying the whole campus because they needed to re-up every few days. Speed would always be the first to go during finals.

The white boys were our best customers, but that changed when one of students overdosed on ecstasy at a dorm party and died on the way to the hospital. The white boys decided to stop selling all together because the chick who overdosed was a good friend of theirs. I couldn't blame them for wanting to quit. They were school boys anyway. They wouldn't have been on the scene much longer. The white boys had no future in the drug game. For them, it was just something to help them get by. We needed more clients, and we needed them quickly.

Word got out in the hood that we were big-time hustlers and a few younger cats wanted to get put on the team. Instinctively, I was against adding new soldiers to the squad, but we had to expand to keep business flowing. Trey and Monster grew up in the same neighborhood as we did and were a couple of years younger. They didn't have the money to get on deck, but they did have ambition. We put Trey and Monster on credit and let them grind it out on their own. They were buying their own supply from us after a few months of hustling in the club scene.

Getting clients that were already established was difficult because they were set in their ways, and if you undercut the competition, you made a new enemy. So, the best way to build an empire was to get our own runners and gunners to put in work for the team.

By the time we had ten young soldiers grinding for us, the team had earned over two hundred fifty thousand dollars. Half of the money was split between James, Black and me, and the other half was re-up money. We bought enough product to supply all of our runners on credit until they could afford to re-up without it.

The goal was to make all of my runners self sufficient, so they would never feel like they were getting cheated. If they weren't making enough, it was all on them. That was the difference between JayBird and me. My team was free to fly alone or stay with the flock. JayBird ran a tight system and that was one of the things that I admired about him most. But if you keep your foot on a man's neck too long, he's bound to struggle for air. He was all about efficiency and not letting anything slip through the cracks because all it takes is one small mistake.

JayBird's clients were in control of the territory on the south side of the city, so my team was clear to hustle there until we started expanding east where the Mexican gangs moved their products and patrolled the streets. One of my runners was robbed at gunpoint on the borderline of the east and south sides of the city by a couple of Mexican bangers when he was meeting with one of his regulars.

The bangers left my runner with a message after stealing about ten thousand dollars worth of product. "Looks like you wandered into the wrong part of town, ese'.

Next time, we'll take your life too." The client disappeared after the run in with the bangers. He said he didn't feel safe doing business with us, but we know we were set up.

It's hard to take a loss, but it's harder to let people get over on you. Revenge was on my mind, but JayBird told us to leave it alone. We were in the middle of a war that had been going on for years.

"Don't try to flush the toilet when you didn't create the shit, Ace."

That sounded like the right thing to do, but if you're already stuck in the war, you might as well defend yourself. I made sure all of my runners were with or near a gunner when making a transaction worth five thousand dollars or more. Whether the customer was a regular or not, we had to take the proper precautions in case the transaction got interrupted by uninvited guests.

Even after trying to prepare for a worst-case scenario, the bangers hit us again when and where we least expected it. Trey and

Monster returned to their apartment complex after doing a transaction one night and heard a frantic knock moments after entering their unit. Monster and Trey looked at each other confusedly; they were a little curious as to who would be knocking on the door right after they walked in.

Monster pulled out a 9mm from his waistband and held the gun behind his back as Trey approached the door and looked through the peephole while asking, "Who is it?" On the other side of the door, Trey saw a young puffy-eyed Latina woman crying, as she mumbled, "I'm sorry to bother you sir, but I really need to use a phone. My boyfriend just hit me and threw me out of the car. I have no idea where I am. Please, sir."

Trey looked at Monster, skeptical and hesitant to open the door, but he finally did. A pretty little lady with tears in her eyes and a red mark across her face stood there trying to hold back tears. Trey opened the door wider for the stranded woman to come in.

"You can come in and get cleaned up if you want, sweetie. The phone is right over there," he said while pointing to a cordless phone mounted to the wall.

When Trey went to close the door, it was kicked open with force as a masked man entered the apartment and let off a round from his Beretta into Trey's chest, making him fall back onto the kitchen floor. Monster let off a couple of rounds from his 9mm, hitting the masked man in the neck, as he instantly slumped over.

Suddenly, bullets from a fully automatic weapon broke the living room window as they traveled through the apartment. Monster hit the floor and rolled towards the wall while sending bullets in the opposite direction. One of the stray bullets from the fully automatic struck the pretty woman between the eyes while she attempted to dodge them, as she ran into the bathroom. Her body fell lifeless.

The gunman with the assault rifle stopped firing and started to reload as he slowly entered the apartment and immediately received a round from Monster's 9mm in the leg as he fell to one knee. Monster pulled the trigger again, click! The masked man smiled and aimed the assault rifle at Monster. BANG! The masked man fell forward with a bullet wedged between his shoulder blade and collarbone. Trey stood over him and emptied the clip into his back.

Somebody had it out for us. We assumed the Eastsiders were responsible but had no real proof they were behind the vicious shoot out and robbery. Trey and Monster got off on a self-defense plea but still did a little time for possession of unregistered firearms. We put our operation on hiatus for a few months to let the heat die down from the shootings. Retaliation was inevitable, and we needed to stay ready for combat. We had a pistol on us every time we left the house because we didn't know who the enemies were. We only knew they could strike at any time.

Before we started moving products again, I decided to do a thorough background check on all of my runners and gunners to make sure the mole wasn't one of the team members.

Black, James and I took the time to monitor each of our team members to see whom they were interacting with other than us. The clients were also potential culprits, so we took the time to investigate an actual connection to the Eastsiders, but we couldn't find anything.

There is a possibility that the activities that took place were just random, but the way they were calculating both times shows they had planned them out. There were two simple rules: never go on a transaction alone and circle the block to make sure you weren't being followed on the drive home. The team didn't run into any issues after the shootout. Whoever was responsible got a dose of karma in three body bags.

Joy got pregnant again with our daughter about a year after we moved into the condo. With another child on the way, I was hustling harder than ever, trying to get ready for my daughter to arrive. The problem was I was hardly home, and that put Joy under a lot of stress not knowing what I was doing or where I was in the world. She constantly worried and accused me of cheating on her. I knew that wasn't good for the baby, so I finally decided to come clean about what I was doing for the past three years to provide for our family.

Joy was angry not only for the fact that I was putting my freedom at risk when we had a two-year-old son and a baby girl on the way, but because I had been lying to her since we met. We tried to work it out, but Joy left me about six months into the pregnancy. When I got home early one morning after being out grinding all night, I found all Joy's belongings missing. The only thing she left was a note on the bed that read:

Ace,

I refuse to be with someone who will put his freedom at risk when he has a family who is dependent upon him. Who knows what you're getting into while out in these streets, Ace? I don't want to be here to get that knock on the door bearing bad news, nor do I want my kids to be in harm's way just because their daddy chooses to live a certain way. I'll be at my parents' house if you need to contact me, or if you feel like spending some time with your son. I'll be waiting for you to change your mind.

Joy

I pleaded for her to reconsider, but she wouldn't unless I was going to stop doing what I was doing to support us. But, I was in too deep to just up and quit. Joy couldn't believe I would choose the street life over my family, but it wasn't about that. I couldn't just up and leave my only source of income without a backup plan. Joy grew to resent me after a couple of months of not changing my ways.

It got to the point where she didn't want me to see Junior at all. Joy was trying everything in the book to get me to change, and I probably wouldn't have been there to see my daughter born if it wasn't for her mom calling me without Joy's permission when she went into labor.

It was hard for me to be in that bedroom all night. I had not slept in that condo since Joy left, and I still couldn't. Black was on the couch asleep when I walked downstairs to pour myself some cognac in a glass. I sat at the dining room table and sipped the liquor with the bottle right next to me for an easy refill. I lit a blunt and took a drag, and I swirled the brown liquid around in the glass.

The aroma was strong because Black stirred awake and smiled at me when he saw me at the dining table puffing the blunt.

"Why didn't you wake me up for breakfast?"

Black joined me at the table, and I passed the blunt to him, then poured him a little cognac. Black took a swig of the drink and said, "Ahh, compliments to the chef." We raised our glass and made a toast.

Black passed the blunt to me and asked, "You couldn't sleep huh?" I shook my head no as I took a drag. Black didn't like seeing me like that. He wasn't used to it.

"Don't worry about nothing, Ace. When we find out who was responsible for this, it's over. We're going to put all of this to and end, big dog. Believe that."

I nodded my head without much enthusiasm. Then James emerged from the guestroom with sleep still in his eyes.

He said, "Black, you loud as a mutha fucka, dog. I came out here to tell you to shut the fuck up, but I guess I'll stay since the blunt is going around."

James joined us at the dining room table and hit the blunt. "What y'all doing up so early? The sun ain't even up yet."

Without answering his question, I blurted out, "I wanna get out the drug game."

James choked hard on the blunt when I said that, and Black couldn't believe what he was hearing. "Hold up. Who are you and what did you do with my homie, Ace?"

I replied, "It's still me. I just had a lot of time to think while I was in the hospital recovering. I keep replaying that night over and over and in my head, and I never want to go through something like that again because next time I might not be so lucky. I never want to see one of you in the position that I'm in right now either. I don't know what I'd do if I actually lost one of you to this game. I've lost too much to this game already. My family is gone, and I'm lucky to be breathing. I can't even see my kids right now because of this."

James seemed to not like my idea. "I understand your concerns, Ace. But, how do you plan on making money 'cuz that's all we've ever done?" I pulled a pamphlet from my back pants' pocket and put it on the table. The pamphlet had "Free Business Start-up Seminar" on the front cover.

Black picked up the pamphlet and read, "Business Start-up?"

I nodded my head 'yes.' "I came across that when I was in the hospital. I think we should invest the money we've made into something legit. I don't want to have to look over my shoulder for the rest of my life. You have no idea how bad I want to get back at whoever did this to me, but I do know that if I keep looking for trouble, I will find it. Or, it will find me. Either way. I'm over it."

I didn't know if James and Black would agree with me on that, but I sure hoped they would. "I know that you don't have to follow my lead on this, but at least go the seminar with me to see what they're talking about. They only have them once a month, and they're having one tonight." Black seemed to be more receptive to the idea than James.

He decided to ask, "What type of business do you want to start?"

I answered with a smile on my face, "A nightclub downtown."

James perked up, "Oh, now you're talking. You've really been thinking about this for a while." James could tell how excited I was about making that move towards something different.

I explained, "I got it all planned out in my head, but I can't do this alone."

Black was the first to agree, "I'm in. You know I got your back."

James wasn't quick to agree, but he didn't go against the grain, "Well, if y'all are in, I'm in. I'm not about to be in these streets solo."

James and Black accompanied me to my therapy session with Dr. Bryant later that afternoon. The usual shenanigans were happening, especially with both of them there, but Dr. Bryant let it slide because I was almost fully recovered. She told me that some of the staff were asking about me and that they missed me even though I had only been gone a day. I was happy to know that so many people truly cared about me and my well-being. I wasn't just another patient.

After leaving the hospital, we headed straight for the seminar, which was being held in the banquet hall of a five-star hotel. When we arrived, the first thing I noticed was we were the only ones who looked out of place.

Everyone there had on business attire and was carrying some type of briefcase, and most had some type of laptop or tablet to take notes with. We didn't even have a pen and paper to write with, and most of the people kept looking us up and down, while snickering and saying things under their breath about us as we passed by.

We took a seat in the front row. I guess they would have preferred for us to sit in the back because one of the staff members had the nerve to come over and ask, "You guys know this is a business seminar, right?" James, Black, and I all looked at each other and raised our eyebrows thinking the same thing. I waited for the moment after the awkward pause to answer.

"No, my friends and I just like to find random banquet rooms to hang out in."

The staff member chuckled emba-rrassingly and walked off without saying anything. When the seminar began, the host walked up to the podium and asked for everyone to quiet down and take their seats. I couldn't help but notice how beautiful the host was. Her caramel skin glowed in the light, and her suit hugged every curve of her body. I punched Black in the arm to see if he was seeing what I saw.

"Bruh, you see what I see?" Black laughed and nodded his head at me as she went on to introduce herself and the main speaker.

"Hello, everyone. Thank you for joining us for this month's start-up business seminar. I'm your host, Lisette, and we have a lot of great topics to go over today. So without further delay, I'd like to introduce our speaker, Mr. Derek Weils."

The audience gave him a warm welcome with a round of applause as Lisette continued speaking. "Mr. Weils was the head of three Fortune 500 companies before he created his own business con-sulting firm. He acquired a Master's in Business from Stanford University and has helped create over fifty millionaires. Please give him a warm welcome."

Derek was dressed to impress in an Italian suit and shoes, and his baritone voice spoke with authority. I learned a lot about the functions of a business working with JayBird in the office. He even taught me how to keep the books, but I never learned how businesses are created. Derek talked a lot about how to start a business, the importance of a well-drawn out business plan, start-up cost, how to find investors, and the best way to pitch your idea to them.

After the seminar, I slowly approached the podium to introduce myself to Derek, but I was intercepted by Lisette, as she said, "Hi, I'm Derek's assistant, if you need anything please let me know." I guess it was my appearance that made her stop me in my tracks, but I wasn't complaining, as long as she was talking to me. Her presence nearly made me forget what I was trying to do before she interrupted me.

"I'm actually looking to invest in a business with money that I made in other ventures, and I really want to get some advice from Mr. Weils," I said.

Derek overheard me talking to Lisette and stepped in to introduce himself while shaking my hand. "Derek Weils. I heard you tell Lisette you want to invest your money into a business. What kind of business?"

"A nightclub, a classy joint downtown," I answered.

Derek smiled and said, "This couldn't have been a more perfect time to meet me. Here's my card. Give me a call on Monday, and we'll talk." Derek handed me one of his business cards and shook my hand again. "Let's talk soon."

Lisette winked at me and gave me one of her cards as well, "You're going to have to go through me to get to him, so you might as well take one of mine too."

VI

After Dr. Bryant had discharged me from the hospital, it took about four months for my body to become fully functional again. When I was one hundred percent recovered, the daily therapy sessions were no longer needed, and I was able to run top speed if the occasion should present itself. Dr. Bryant is my hero and will always be one of the most important persons in my life.

She was always modest about her heroism saying, "I'm just doing my job, Ace. Just the same as any other doctor would." Deep down inside, she knew how special she was to me despite the fact she downplayed herself every time I told her that she knew magic.

"You sure you're not some kinda wizard, Doc?" I asked her every time I had a chance to.

The condo had become home ever since the break in. Playing it safe made more sense than blatantly putting myself in harm's way for my enemies' convenience. I installed surveillance cameras around the property and a screen in every room of the house, in case the assailants found me. The safety on my Beretta was never on these days. I even left my pistol on the sink when I showered with the curtain cracked just enough for me to see the surveillance screen.

Constant paranoia made carrying out daily business routines a new difficult task. The night I got shot was on repeat in my mind every time I tried to make moves. Miracles are phenomena that go far beyond human comprehension. The universe spared my life and offered me another chance to right my wrongdoings. Something died in me the night I got shot. The tragedy rebirthed my existence and redirected my path onto something positive.

The part of me that died that night was holding onto the pain from hardships and trials I encountered during my adolescent years. Once that part of me was buried six feet underground, an unbearable weight was lifted off my shoulders, and the anger I constantly suppressed no longer had a hold on my sanity. My outlook on life changed completely, as I finally realized how much my actions affected not just me but my loved ones as well as the addicts.

Business proceeded without a glitch when I was recovering because James and Black were still hustling. I don't know what I would do if either of them were in my shoes. Pre-incident guilt put a lump in my throat when I thought about either of them laid up in the hospital from an attempted murder. Even though we are all free to make our own choices in life, the fact that I put James and Black on the team would make me feel partially responsible if something tragic happened to either of them due to our line of work.

For the most part, our operation could run itself without me being there. I trust my boys with my life and know they wouldn't do me dirty. The operation ran like clock-work, almost as if that night never happened. But even though business was still booming, my presence was missed in the streets. My runners would often come to me for guidance and advice, or if they just needed someone to talk to when they were having baby mama drama. Most of the team was already intact when Joy and I were going through the worst part of our relationship, so the expert advice they received was invaluable.

Other than my family, the team was everything to me. I treated my employees like royalty because they were valuable assets to my business. An unhappy employee who is feeling spiteful can bring down the whole operation in the blink of an eye. That's why my runners and gunners got paid top dollar for their services. No one on my team got cheated because I didn't have real employees.

What I built was a network of leaders who all worked together for a common goal. We were a tight-knit family of ambitious individuals who made the team their life. We even had Sunday dinner and our weekly meetings at Big Mama's Soul Food Kitchen. Our table was always reserved and waiting for us when we arrived every week. We had to be their favorite customers because they treated us like celebrities when we walked through the door.

My team still had their weekly meetings and Sunday dinner when I was in the hospital. I made sure they stayed on track, so they wouldn't slip up and end up like me. Big Mama sent a plate to the hospital every week when she got news about the incident. She wrote a note every week on one side of the paper to-go bag for me to read. One of the notes read:

"Next time, I'm going to make you get your butt out that hospital bed to get a

plate. I know how much you love my cooking. Maybe it will motivate you to get out that bed and walk again."

Big Mama's food and thoughtful messages were a great reminder that everyone was not against me during a time I could only trust a handful of people. Her gesture made me feel compassion towards others when I started to suspect any and everyone to be a potential enemy. Big Mama knew she was killing me with kindness when my heart was black and cold for answers and revenge.

The Sunday I went back to Big Mama's, my mobility was fully recovered. I didn't want my team to see me when my condition was anything less than what they were used to. They needed to stay focused on staying safe in the streets, and seeing their leader weak would only affect the team negatively, because you are only as strong as your weakest link. Even if that weakest link is the leader, he must know when to remove himself from the playing field for the well-being of the team, so I let James and Black lead, so I could recover properly.

The damage was deep mentally and physically. Seeing me in a wheelchair would have sent the team on a downward spiral. Either they were going to get scared for their own lives and start making serious mistakes in the street, or they would be out seeking revenge on the unknown shooter. Either one of those would have brought unneeded heat towards the squad. The best bet was for me to lay low until the situation blew over and I was well again.

Black and James helped me surprise the team at Big Mama's for dinner. They distracted them at the table, so no one noticed when I walked up with one of the restaurant's aprons and ball caps on, pretending to be a waiter saying, "You niggas are here every week, and you still don't know what you want yet do you?"

Trey looked up at me with an expression that said, "What the fuck?" When he noticed it was me, he stood up and grabbed me like a relative who lived out of state. Trey's voice was loud and excited, "Oh shit! Ace!?" The rest of the team at the table jumped up and greeted me with the same respect that they would give to the oldest elder in the family.

Monster was noticeably overwhelmed with emotion when he hugged me like a brother and said, "Happy to have you back boss man. These streets haven't been the same since you've been gone. But, we're still out here taking care of business for you. The team ain't going nowhere."

The warm welcome made me feel like I was at home again, and Big Mama's kitchen gave off a familiar aroma that made my mouth salivate and my taste buds tingle with anticipation. Our table was in a section designated for parties in the back of the restaurant, so we could talk business without questioning if people were ear hustling. Plus, Big Mama let us pop a couple of bottles of champagne even though she didn't serve alcohol on a normal basis.

That day was a special occasion. We celebrated my return to the team and my recovery after nearly being murdered in cold blood. We all raised our glasses to toast when one of our runners named Mac decided to take the mic, "Let's make a toast to, Ace, for being a bad ass mother fucker. None of us would be in this room and most of us would be flat broke if it wasn't for you. So, I'm speaking for all of us when I say, you da man."

After being in the hospital and away from the team for nearly a year, I felt closer to them than ever before. My team was not a team anymore. We truly became a family that hustled together without questioning another's loyalty. This was the only family that I never screwed up from being something less than what they desired. My team looked up to me. They respected me. I respected them. I treated them well. We all earned money, and everybody was happy. But things were going to change soon, and the feeling was bittersweet when I thought about all good things coming to an end.

Big Mama fed us until our bellies were packed tightly with food for the soul. We had finished four bottles of champagne when I decided to break the news to the team. I tapped my champagne glass with a butter knife to capture everyone's attention at the table. They all turned towards me, and I waited for silence before speaking.

"Y'all have no idea how much this team means to me. I consider each and every one of you family, because that's what we've grown to be. You don't need the same blood to be related. You need loyalty and trust. All of you have proved that you are worthy of this family at some point in time, and your sincerity is recognized and appreciated. With that being said, I unfortunately have to announce that I'm getting out of the game forever. The money might be good, but it's not worth your life gentlemen. First, it was Trey and Monster; then, they tried to get me. Who's next? It's only a matter of time before this happens again, and I don't want to see any of you in the same situation I was in, or worse. I know this is sudden, but I've thought long and hard, so don't try to fight me on this."

The team stayed quiet for a few moments, shocked at the news they just received as they tried to digest the information with their collard greens. One of the runners named C-Note responded first saying, "So, that's it? You're done just like that? What about us? What are we supposed to do?" The looks on their faces ranged from anger to confusion, and some were disappointed in reaction to the news. It was hard to watch your empire crumble after so many years of hard work from your team, but it's harder to see a life taken away over money, and I didn't get into this business to be a grim reaper.

C-Note's questions were valid concerns, but dropping the whole team without warning after everything we went through would be a faulty move on my part. I tried my best to address the questions and clarify my plans.

"No, I'm not done just like that. I plan on getting one more shipment of products for y'all, but after that it'll be your choice to continue and build another team, or you can quit. I'm positive you all made enough to be your own man, so you would never have to rely on me. I know all of you can keep swimming when I take away the life vests, and you didn't even know you were learning how to swim this entire time."

A few of the guys nodded their heads in agreement after I explained the situation. Then, Mac broke the silence and asked, "So, what do you plan on doing after all of this is over? What's next?"

For some reason, my whole mood unexpectedly changed when I thought about a future without being a young kingpin, always looking in the rearview mirror and over my shoulder.

"I'm going to take the money I made and invest in a nightclub/restaurant where I'll be one of the partners. I've been working on this deal since I was discharged from the hospital about four months ago, and we're on the verge of closing and finalizing the documents. But when we do, our doors will be open to anyone of you who wants to get out of the game and start a new chapter in life. Y'all are like family, but I'm not going to tell you what to do with your life."

Most of the team understood where I was coming from and nodded in agreement, but Cloud 9, one of the youngest on the team decided to start conflict and said, "You know what? What was the point of you coming back?"

Black started to refrain him from speaking up, "What the fuck? Who do you think you are to be questioning anybody about…."

I interrupted Black to save the child from the wrath. "Let him speak, Black. We're all entitled to our own opinion."

Cloud 9 spoke in a less aggressive tone when he asked, "I mean, how are you gonna just drop us like that? You come in here talking about family, loyalty and honesty and then pull a stunt like this when you knew four months ago that you were leaving us for good. That's not loyalty or honesty, so how can you call us family?"

Cloud 9 got up and walked out of the restaurant fuming. Black started to stop him, but I interrupted him again.

"Let him go, Black. He's too young to see what we see. Maturity is something you can't teach."

Black snarled; he was agitated by the teen's outburst. "I got something that will teach him to shut his mouth. Little fucker was out of line."

What Cloud 9 had said was somewhat true even if he was out of line. I guess the team was a family to others as well and to hear that we had plans to break that union did not sit well with those who didn't have anything to fall back on. Cloud 9 didn't have any biological family around, so the team was the closest thing to a family he knew for the last four years.

There wasn't anything I could think of to transition from the subject of leaving the business after Cloud 9 disrupted the meeting. Everyone at the table was in his own little world anyway trying to collect his thoughts and make plans to prepare for our last shipment as he weighed out all of his options.

Getting out of the game and setting up a business deal with Mr. Weils was my main focus, and nothing was going to get in the way of that. Any of my team members were welcome to come join the new hustle. I wasn't forcing anything on them, but if they chose to come to the club, they would forfeit that other lifestyle on the side. My business could not be associated with anything pertaining to my old lifestyle. Everything had to be legit. No one could cut corners or make side money, unless he wanted to find himself on the side of the road unemployed.

JayBird only came to visit me once at the hospital. He found out I was there because he knew something was wrong when my regular order wasn't placed as usual. After a couple of days, JayBird reached out to Black and got the news about me being shot. He immediately rushed to the hospital to check on me.

Ten years had passed since I started my own operation and become one of JayBird's clients, and a couple of years after I left the nest, I was his best client, and he wasn't surprised at my success.

"I gotta keep an eye on you. You're gonna be aiming for my job soon." JayBird was joking, but you could hear he was halfway serious. We grew apart over the years, but I still thought of JayBird as a big brother who saved me from myself when I was a lost soul in my early teens.

Normally, I would call JayBird on the phone and make my order talking in a code he created for his clients. Anyone who broke the code was cut off indefinitely. "Better safe and broke than careless behind bars and still broke." JayBird preached that saying at least once a week when I worked the graveyard shift at the warehouse. That time around, a trip to the warehouse was necessary because what I had to say couldn't be spoken in code. Plus, what I had to say was something that had to happen face to face.

JayBird was on the phone like always when I entered his office at the warehouse, having another heated discussion with one of his employees.

"Look, I don't know what's going on in that brain of yours, but those are company trucks and company gas, so stop going on personal runs during your shift…. and the next time you want to lie about it, McKinsey, remember all company vehicles are equipped with GPS."

The way JayBird constantly stayed on his employees' asses you would think his name was Levi. When JayBird hung up the phone, he showed me love like he thought he'd never see me again.

"You're one of the strongest dudes I know. Somebody shoulda warned those fucking cowards: You're fucking with the wrong one. They better stay in hiding because if we ever find 'em, they're gonna get put back in the hole they crawled out of."

Hearing JayBird speak about vengeance gave me anxiety. Finding out who was holding the gun that shot me was more important because they were most likely still on the loose and could pop whenever they pleased. I kept a .38 special in a pocket holster at all times; in case, we should meet again.

After a little small talk, I told JayBird about my plans to retire from the drug game and how life had given me a second chance, so I wanted to do something positive with the grands I had made.

"Most of the time, they tell you to quit while you're ahead, and seeing that I'm alive today, I would consider that being ahead. I had a good run, made some money, and now it's time to move onto the next stage." I was straight to the point.

JayBird adsorbed the information with a silent straight face, and after I was done, he simply replied, "This business ain't for everyone. You did more in less time than most cats do in a lifetime. You gotta know when to hold 'em and when to fold 'em. I trust you as long as you trust yourself. I've had your back since day one, so I'm behind whatever decision you make."

I placed the biggest order of my career with JayBird seeing that it would be my last. I wanted to leave my team with enough product to last them for a while, just in case they needed more time to figure out what they wanted to do next. My team was there for me every step of the way, and I didn't want to leave them without making sure they were able to stay afloat until they could find another connect.

JayBird didn't trust a lot of people and only wanted the products to be shipped to me. Then, I would distribute them to the rest of team. He wasn't open to referrals because you never know who someone was bringing into the network, and it was a risk he was not willing to take. If any of my team wanted to keep hustling in the streets, they would have to find their own connect for inventory.

The last shipment arrived the next day, and I picked it up at the P.O. Box with Black and James. We fell back to the condo to separate and repackage what we were going to send out to the team. They all were getting enough to last them approximately three months after my planned retirement. James sparked up a blunt and took a drag while we sat at the dining room table working.

"I can't believe this is it. We're about to be officially out of the game, gentlemen."

James passed the blunt to Black, as he gave his two cents about the situation. "Well, it's not like we were going to stay in the game forever. Nobody stays in forever. We know that."

I jumped in, "We got bigger and better things to move on to. Trust me."

My cell phone rang right after Black passed the blunt to me. Monster was on the other end yelling frantically in my ear.

"Yo, Boss. You need to get down here asap, man. They got Cloud 9 and C-Note last night. They did 'em cold blooded. I ain't neva seen no shit like this before, Ace."

By the time James, Black and I arrived to the scene, it was swarming with black and white squad cars and forensics detectives. The shopping center was roped off with yellow caution tape, so there was no way any of us was going to get near the scene. C-Notes' car was parked in one of the stalls, as the police searched through the vehicle for evidence. C-Note and Cloud 9's bodies lay lifeless under white sheets next to the driver and passenger doors.

The shattered glass from the driver's and passenger's windows suggested they were ambushed from both sides and probably never had a chance to survive the attack or defend themselves. We saw one of the detectives pull out a 9mm from under the front passenger seat. They were prepared, just not ready for what they encountered.

My stomach suddenly turned, and I felt the need to vomit, so I pushed open the passenger door and let my lunch go. The sight was too much for me at the moment, and Black pulled off before we brought any attention to ourselves as he asked, "You alright, Ace." I nodded my head and wiped the corners of my mouth as we pulled off to meet with Monster and the rest of the team just a few blocks away.

We pulled over to the side of the road where we saw the rest of the team waiting for us. I immediately jumped out of the car to demand answers. "Who did this?" None of them had an answer for me, and it bothered me even more "Speak dammit! Nobody knows shit?" They all shook their heads, unable to produce any answers.

"Somebody is out to get us. It is obvious. They're going to try and get us all one by one," said James.

It was a fact that all of us then knew, but no one wanted to say. I wanted to walk away from the game, but somebody wasn't going to make it easy for me. They wanted war, and I wasn't about to let my soldiers get killed off without doing anything about it.

I started making orders to the team. "Everybody get strapped up, and don't go anywhere alone until we can figure out who is targeting us. We're not making any more drops until further notice. I mean it. No moves until I say so. I got some shit to handle, so we're not moving shit until I get back. You hear me? No moves!"

The team stayed silent for a moment but eventually agreed to my demands. Most of them looked heated enough to light a wild fire, but I didn't want them to do anything stupid to jeopardize themselves or the rest of the team.

I had to meet with Derek at his office to finalize some paperwork later that evening, and my nerves were getting the best of me. The image of Cloud 9 and C-Note lying on the pavement was stuck in my mind. I didn't realize Derek was trying to get my attention until Lisette put a hand on my shoulder and shook me back to reality.

"Mr. Johnson. Are you okay? We've been trying to get your attention for the last couple of minutes."

I nodded my head, "Yes, I'm sorry. I'm fine. It's just been a really long and strange day. That's all."

Derek jumped in, "Are you having seconds thoughts about this, Ace? You sure you want to do this?"

"Mr. Weils, I've never been more sure about anything in my life. It's just I have a lot going on in my personal life right now. That's all. But it's nothing that's going to stop us from opening up this club as planned."

Derek shuffled around some papers on his desk. "Well, Ace, everything is still going to go as we agreed to, and I know all of this paperwork can be a little stressful. Why don't you let my lawyers take care of the rest of the contract negotiations for you? When we reach a common ground, we will finalize the paperwork. Then, you can come in and sign off on everything. Until then, I think it is important for you to take care of whatever is bothering you. It is more important to take of yourself right now. Leave the rest of this to us."

I was appreciative of Derek's offer. My mind was in a different place at the moment, and they could sense there was something seriously wrong, as I couldn't concentrate on what they were saying for more than a few moments before drifting off into lala land. I agreed to let them handle the paperwork, and I proceeded to leave Derek's office for the night.

Lisette decided to walk me out. I figured she was going to try and get some info out of me, and she did.

"I've never seen you like this before, Mr. Johnson. Are you sure everything is fine?"

I started to lie to her, but I truthfully stated, "No, everything's not fine, but I'm hoping that it will be soon. I just have a few things to take care of."

Lisette placed her hand over my heart as if she knew what was going on and said, "Well, if you ever need anything, or you just want someone to talk to just know that I'm here for you okay. You have my number. Don't hesitate to call me."

James and Black had waited outside Derek's office during the brief meeting. We needed to stay close to each other just in case any of us were being targeted. We weren't taking any chances at that point, especially after what they did to the lil' homies Cloud 9 and C-Note.

VII

The way Cloud 9 and C-Note were executed filled the team with rage and disbelief. When I showed up to Monster and Trey's place with Black and James in the dark of the early morning, the team was preparing enough artillery to start a small war as they loaded more weaponry than all of us could carry on us at once. The team was ready for battle against an army of ghosts. Our enemies were good at staying anonymous; whoever they were, in our eyes, they were cowards and needed to be stopped before they tried to take out another soldier on the team.

"So nobody knows anything?" I demanded answers as soon as I walked inside the house. The whole team shrugged their shoulders and shook their heads, clueless as to whom we were ready to wage war upon. Monster stood up with his face bawled tight like a fist and pumped the shotgun that was clinched in his hands.

"Whomever it is, they're going to pay," growled Monster. "Nine and Note were just getting started, too fresh in the game to get gunned down like kingpins. They haven't put in enough work to gain that type of reputation and hate. They didn't deserve what these pussies deserve." Monster's analysis on the situation made sense,

"Word must be out that I'm still alive," I concluded. "They want us spooked and making mistakes, so they can catch the rest of us slippin'."

Even if I wanted to walk away from the game, at that point there was no way I would ever feel safe knowing there were people out there who wanted to wipe out my team. I sat at the dining room table to collect my thoughts when my cell phone rang; I accepted the call when JayBird's name popped up on the caller ID. His temper was out of control as he shouted into the phone furiously.

"Ace, I heard about what happened to your boys last night. I think I know who did it. Meet me at the warehouse, and bring two of your best men."

The news made my heart jump with anxiety before pressing the end button. I started barking orders like a drill sergeant, "James, Black, strap up. That was Bird; he said he got some answers for us. We might be putting in work tonight."

The rest of the team fell in line and filled their holsters with weapons until I stopped them in their tracks.

"I need y'all to hold down the spot for now. James and Black are the only two rolling with me."

Trey stepped up and cocked his pistol ready for conflict as he barked, "What you mean, Ace? Cloud 9 and C-Note was like family to us too. If you're on a mission, all of us are on a mission. We ride together; we die together."

Trey's loyalty to the team was admirable. The fire in his eyes ignited the rest of the team into action. Chucky stood up and tucked a gun into his waistband. "Yea, we ride together; we die together." He repeated the motto while looking at me with the same fire in his eyes. Even if I wanted the rest of the team with me, two people meant two people. More soldiers meant taking chances that could compromise the mission because the team wanted to settle personal vendettas, and that's when the shit hits the fan.

JayBird's words were burned into my brian: "Don't take business personally. That's how your personal business gets com-promised. Leave all those emotions and hang ups at the door, and you'll find success in both aspects of your life."

Even though we all considered the team to be like family, this was a business call that could be compromised by taking what happened to Cloud 9 and C-Note personally. Revenge was on my mind, but what I wanted more than anything was the identity of the cowards who were targeting us. That was the most vital objective.

I pulled rank for the sake of the team's well-being. "Look, I know y'all want to put in work for Cloud 9 and C-Note, but be smart about it and listen to me. Stay here and hold down the spot. Keep your eyes and ears open just in case we need to call for backup. Can all of you do that for me?" The team reluctantly agreed and sat back down disarming themselves, with their bravado deflated, as the three of us walked out on a mission.

The violet night sky shifted to a pale grey as the light of day gradually approached us when we arrived to the warehouse. JayBird wasn't in his office as usual. He met us at the front door and invited us inside before I was able to ring the bell.

"Hurry up. Get in here. Nobody followed you here right?" asked JayBird. He poked his head out of the door after we came inside to double check.

"Of course not. I know the rules," I reassured JayBird as he closed the door behind him. JayBird didn't resemble the person I was used to dealing with. Instead of being calm and collected, he looked like a nervous wreck as he paced a short distance back and forth rubbing his goatee repeatedly for increased wisdom.

The three of us stood there and waited patiently for JayBird to address us. He stopped in his tracks and gave us a once over. "Seems like you three are inseparable. You don't find that type of bond between homies too often. Last time I saw this one, he wasn't old enough to hold his liquor," said JayBird as he pointed at James. The memory of James being drunk at the party I met JayBird at made the salty moment slightly sweeter. We looked at each other and managed to crack a smile.

"They're not my homies, Jay. They're my brothers," I said in correction to his comment.

"That's good. Don't let anything or anyone break that bond. You're stronger as a team. It's loyalty before royalty. Remember that." JayBird preached the truth, but I was anxious to get down to business.

"You alright, Jay? I've never seen you like this," my question came from a place of sincere concern.

"No, I'm not okay," JayBird replied honestly. "The graveyard shift got hit last night. They came through the emergency escape tunnels and got us for the whole supply. Come on. I want y'all to see the surveillance tape."

We followed JayBird up to his office and stood behind the desk as he sat in his chair and grabbed the remote from the top drawer. He pointed the remote at the receiver under the surveillance screen and punched in a four-digit code. The screen blacked out and then switched to a view of four different camera angles on the lower level. "Watch this shit," said JayBird as he hit rewind on the remote and then play after reaching 3:16am on the time display. As the video played, the footage we watched displayed a normal night on the graveyard shift as employees weighed and packaged outgoing products.

The operation moved like a well-oiled machine until an unexpected explosion blasted two small steel doors attached to the back wall clear off their hinges across the room. Workers scrambled out of the way like dodge ball players. The guard posted in back of the room met one of the steel doors face first. His body went flimsy like a sock puppet as the door knocked him unconscious. The guard at the main entrance tried to train his uzzi through the smoke and debri when he was shot twice in the torso. His legs buckled under him as the gun went off and shot out a florescent bulb that was mounted to the ceiling.

Two men emerged from each door and invaded the room wearing all black ski masks, hoodies, pants and tactical boots. One of the men carried an M-16 assault rifle. One was equipped with a double-barrel sawed-off shotgun, and two held 9mm pistols. They all carried large black duffel bags over their shoulders.

The armed robbers instructed the employees to line up on the wall. Two of them trained guns on the staff while the other two bound the employees' hands behind their backs with zip ties, then directed them to sit with their legs crossed facing the wall. The thug holding the assault rifle kept an eye on the employees as the other three stuffed the duffle bags with the products that were being processed on the assembly line.

The thug with the shotgun smashed several ceramic sculptures to gut the insides for the product. The ski-masked men emptied the inventory into their duffle bags before disappearing into the dark tunnels, leaving the employees sitting on the floor still bound by the hands but unharmed.

JayBird stopped the video and the screen went black. The video was hard for him to watch as he rubbed his temples with his thumb and index finger to relieve the tension in his head.

"One hundred thousand dollars worth of inventory, gone," JayBird spoke in an unenthusiastic tone. "At least nobody was killed. My guard Tank is in the ICU, but the doctors said he should pull through."

"That's some fucked up shit, Jay. Whoever did this knows the place well," I spoke on an obvious but important observation. JayBird stood up from his leather office chair and leaned over the mahogany desk with his fists holding him up.

He looked me in the eyes and said, "A couple employees said they thought they recognized one of their voices. One was almost certain she heard Fast Lane's voice behind one of those masks. She said she wouldn't mistake the raspiness of the voice that constantly agitated her with unreciprocated flirting."

"Fast Lane!?" Saying the name gave me a nasty taste in my mouth. The bitterness made me spit out the words. "That piece of shit is still around? I thought that problem was taken care of years ago."

JayBird started pacing the length of his desk. "I should have put that scum in the dirt when I had the chance." The anger was noticeable as he raised the volume.

"But, I wanted my money back from all of the product he stole from me: forty grand for the product and forty for interest. I told him I'd go after his family if he didn't pay up, but I only saw ten grand before he disappeared. After two years of waiting and searching, I had a little talk with his folks, either they were going to give me information on his whereabouts or settle the debt for him. They rented their house out and moved a couple of cities away in response, thinking I couldn't find them. When I found them, I had few thugs ransack their place and spray paint, 'Fast Lane ain't quick enough to run from debt,' on their living room wall. They ended up selling one of their houses to settle Lane's debt, so I got all of my money back about three years ago. That grimy snakeskin would have never been let in my circle if I knew he was two-faced."

The information was news to me. I never would have thought Fast Lane would still be a problem after ten years, but I didn't know he was in that deep with JayBird. If JayBird had not decided to put me on the graveyard shift, Fast Lane might have never been caught stealing. He probably thought of me as a snitch, but I wasn't about to let anyone get over on JayBird, especially if I was being held accountable for any slipups.

Time was of the essence. Fast Lane was on the loose looking for payback. He was meticulous when plotting against us, and every move seemed to be calculated. "How are we going to find him? His parents aren't worth enough collateral damage. We all know snakes are cold blooded." We immediately started devising a scheme.

"Does he have any kids? If that doesn't break him, nothing will," suggested James. James was onto something, but Black was skeptical about it and spoke up.

"I don't know what you're getting at J, but I'm not kidnapping any kids."

James clarified what he meant: "I'm not talking about kidnapping the kid, not exactly at least. Trust me, my nigga."

JayBird jumped in, "His baby's mama's name is Raquel. She lives about an hour north of us with their son. I hired a private investigator to pull up everything he could find on Fast Lane when he disappeared. The kid should be at least four years old now."

The plot was beginning to thicken. I asked JayBird, "When are we heading out?"

"Tonight," he answered. "We'll head out at dusk. I have to make sure things are tight around here before the morning staff comes in. Just make sure you're here by sunset."

Before leaving the warehouse, we finished plotting a detailed mission with military precision. I was nervous and excited at the same time, but most of all, I was ready for action. I was ready for revenge.

None of us slept a wink that day as we fell back to the condo to wait for dusk; James and Black sat at the kitchen table drinking cognac and rolling blunts. I tried to join them a couple of times, but nervous energy made me pace around the house, unloading and reloading my Beretta over a thousand times to keep myself busy. The rest of the team was still at Monster and Trey's spot waiting for some feedback. They were still in the dark about what happened at the warehouse and our mission at dusk.

We met JayBird at the warehouse, just as the sun traveled over the horizon. Black drove his SUV. The limo tint made us incognito, and he switched the license plates with a bogus set of dealership plates that he paid a crackhead to steal from a used car lot. JayBird hopped out of the backseat of another SUV that was already in the lot and parked his butt in the backseat of Black's vehicle.

"Those are my goons. They're going to follow behind and keep an eye on us in case shit gets ugly," explained JayBird. "Get on the interstate 420 going north, and remember what we talked about earlier today. Stick to the plan. No brash decisions."

By the time we arrived to Raquel's neighborhood, the night had fully set in. The houses in the small town were spread far apart, and the only light on the street was provided by residential properties, not by the streetlights that we were used to. We finally reached our destination and scoped out the scene for nosey neighbors before exiting the SUV.

"I'll knock on the door. Just make sure you stay in the shadows until I'm in. We don't want her to get spooked," JayBird spoke quietly for stealth.

JayBird crept up to the door of the modest one-story home as the rest of us waited just around the side of the house. He rang the doorbell in a rapid motion and knocked continuously in a panicky manner.

Moments later, we heard a female's voice come from the other side of the door, "What is it? What's going on?"

JayBird's voice rang out in urgency. "Hey, is this your car in the driveway? It's on fire. Hurry up!"

"What!?" Raquel shrieked and unlocked the door to open it swiftly. In the same movement, JayBird rammed the door open with his shoulder and entered the house. Raquel screamed in horror, but the sound was muted when JayBird put his hand over her mouth and drew the gun from under his arm as James, Black, and I ran in after him and shut the door.

JayBird put the gun up to his lips and said, "Shhhhh. Calm down. We're not here to hurt you. Just settle on down now." Raquel listened and stopped screaming, but she couldn't stop herself from crying in fear. JayBird removed his hand from her mouth, and she tried to catch her breath when another high-pitched scream suddenly came from behind and startled us. Fast Lane's son stood at the end of the hallway in Spiderman pajamas screaming to the top of his lungs in terror. "Get him," ordered JayBird, as he motioned for Raquel to go to her son.

Raquel ran over to her son to calm him down. "It's okay, baby. You don't have to be afraid. These are just some of mommy's old friends. I was screaming because they surprised me." She wiped tears away from his face as he started to chill out, but he knew something was wrong as he stared us down studying the features of our faces. "Go back to bed, honey. I'll be there in a little while to tuck you in. Okay?"

We let the little boy walk back into the room before continuing with business. Raquel spoke before we could.

"So what do you want? Money? Jewelry? You can take whatever I have, but it's not much. You might be disappointed that you picked this house."

JayBird cut her off, "We're not here to rob you, lady. We're here to get in touch with your good for nothing baby daddy Fast Lane."

Raquel rolled her eyes and shook her head in disbelief. "He doesn't live here, never did. I don't know where he's staying. We haven't spoke in over a week now."

"We know. That's why you're going to make him come to us," demanded JayBird.

"You're going to call him and tell him his son is sick and he needs to go to the ER asap and your car won't start."

Raquel asked suspiciously, "What are you going to do to him?"

"That's not your concern. Just do as you are told and call him." JayBird's answer diverted her question.

Raquel became defiant, "And what if I don't?" JayBird chuckled and shook his head to disapprove.

"Didn't I tell you we're not here to hurt you? We have a score to settle with Fast Lane. Don't be stupid trying to have his back. If you value your son's life more than Fast Lane's, you'll make the call."

"You wouldn't," Raquel challenged him. "He's just a child."

"Make the call, Raquel, and put it on speaker phone." JayBird's tone suggested he wasn't going to tell her again.

Raquel snarled and grabbed her cell-phone from the kitchen counter. She pressed a few buttons on the keypad. It started to ring after she dialed out.

"What?" Fast Lane's voice blared out of the speaker.

"What do you mean 'What?' That's how you answer the phone when the mother of your son is calling you?" Raquel was fed up, and it showed.

"What do you want, Raquel?" he asked again.

"Your son is sick. He needs to go the ER, and my car won't start," she explained.

"Why you always calling me with some bullshit, like I'm just supposed to stop my life at the drop of a dime and be Superman? You can't find another way to get him there? I'm a little busy right now."

The music in the background was almost as loud as he was. Raquel was used to dealing with that. She cut the crap and asked directly, "You coming or not, ass-hole?"

Fast Lane was thoroughly annoyed, "Fuuuckk. Fine. Yes. I'll be there," he answered before hanging up the phone in her face. Raquel was embarrassed that we all had to hear that.

We all stayed quiet feeling sorry for her until she broke the silence and asked, "You happy now?"

JayBird answered, "More than I show, and more than you know."

Almost two hours passed before a beefed-up custom racecar slid into the driveway with the engine growling like a threatening lioness. It was ironic how it took someone named Fast Lane so long to show up in an emergency situation, especially in a car that barely looked street legal. JayBird and James waited in the hallway while Black and I stood behind the front door.

When Fast Lane walked into the house, Black pistol whipped him in the back of the head and knocked him out like a heavyweight. I closed the door and locked it; then, I proceeded to help Black search Fast Lane for weapons. We pulled out a .45 from his waist and a .22 from his ankle holster. We sat his limp body up in a chair and zip tied his hands behind his back, before splashing ice cold water on his face to bring him back to reality.

Fast Lane gasped for air as he regained consciousness, shook the excess water off of his face, and attempted to focus his blurry vision.

"Morning, sunshine," JayBird greeted a confused Fast Lane with a smile. "Did you miss me?"

Fast Lane blinked his eyes trying to see clearly. He looked at all of us strangely, trying to put the pieces of his memory back together. He squinted his eyes as his brain began to function normally again. JayBird got up close to Fast Lane and stared him square in the face. Fast Lane flinched like he saw a ghost, and his eyes popped open.

"Try not to look so happy to see us," said JayBird as he taunted Fast Lane for amusement.

"You bitch! I can't believe you set me up after everything we've been through," Fast Lane cursed Raquel from across the room. "Just wait till I get loose and…"

"And what? Huh?" I interrupted Fast Lane. "You ain't gonna do shit. She made a choice: her son or you. I'm sure you're not surprised at her decision. Considering the way you spoke to her on the phone, I'm surprised she's not on our side."

Fast Lane grimaced. His demeanor mimicked that of a man with a guilty conscience. His eyes moved in a sketchy pattern, and his breathing was heavy. He questioned JayBird, "What do you want with me now, Bird? My old man told me he already paid you off. I don't owe you jack shit. Let me go!"

JayBird laughed loudly. "He said let me go! Yea, I'll let you go…. to hell." JayBird laughed hard again at his own joke and bumped fists with me.

Fast Lane squirmed around in the chair trying to release himself from the restraints. "Come on, man. What the fuck y'all want with me? Huh?"

JayBird sat a chair directly in front of Fast Lane's and stared him straight in the eyes. "You're like a parasite that embedded himself into my life and won't get the fuck out. No matter how hard I try to kill off the situation, you somehow find a way to crawl back into my life and make it a living hell. Maybe, I need to exterminate the pest instead of eliminating it from the colony. Then, maybe I can be free from an annoying, grotesque pest who's always in my shit. Literally."

Fast Lane shook his head disagreeing, "I'd say it's the other way around Bird. You told me you wanted me gone, so I left. Then, you harassed my parents and made them sell their house. Now, you're breaking into the home where my child lives. If anybody is a pest, it's you. You fucking vampire. Draining the life out of everyone around you to help yourself when you claim to help others. Yea, I got over on you a few times, but I was only getting what I deserved for constantly putting my neck on the line for you. 'I got you, Lane. You gonna get yours; just be patient.' How long am I supposed to be patient? I put in work for you for eight years and never got mine like you promised. So, I took mine. Then, you had this young nigga, Ace, come in to babysit us, having it easy and making more money than all of us in the lab. Little nigga didn't even know how turn on the scale, and you had him running shit? If that's not a slap in the face, I don't know what is."

JayBird wasn't expecting Fast Lane to go on a rant, but he listened intently to every word. When he finished, JayBird said, "I should have left your broke ass on the corner where I found you, pushing nickels and dimes like a chump."

Fast Lane responded, "You're right. That was better than being one of the little bitches you try to keep on a leash."

JayBird was tired of debating with Fast Lane, so he said, "I tell you about these ungrateful mutha fuckas', thinking they're entitled to shit that's not theirs. That's a fucked up way of thinking, Lane. It's what got you into the mess you're in now. Be grateful, not hateful. Somebody is always going to have something that you want and don't have. But if you focus on what you don't have, how can you ever appreciate what's already in your possession? The answer: You can't. That's your problem, Lane; you always got your sights set on something that's not meant for you to have. I know you, Lane. That's how I know you and your goons broke into the warehouse last night and shot Tank, then robbed me with your bitch ass homies. Ain't that right, Fast Lane?

Fast Lane avoided eye contact and looked toward the floor. "I don't know what you're talking about, Bird," he mumbled.

JayBird tried to follow Fast Lane's gaze to maintain eye contact. "Oh, you don't know what I'm talking about? I think you do, Lane. I think you know exactly what I'm talking about."

Fast Lane finally made eye contact with JayBird and stared him in the eyes while saying, "Like I said the first time. I don't know what the fuck you're talking about."

JayBird cracked a smile, finding Fast Lane's denial humorous. "You know, next time you rob a place where the people know who you are, you should think about how distinctive your voice is and shut the fuck up. I never had another person on the squad with a voice like yours, and seeing that you knew exactly how to get in, all fingers point to you."

Fast Lane looked like a deer in the headlights when JayBird confronted him. All he could do was shake his head.

JayBird continued interrogating Fast Lane. "We know you killed Ace's boys. We know you tried to kill Ace, Monster, and Trey too." Fast Lane looked at me like he saw a ghost.

"Y'all are taking this too far now, JayBird. First, you accuse me of robbing you at gunpoint. Now, you're accusing me of murder? You niggas are crazy. There's no proof that I did any of that. My hands are clean. Keep searching because I'm not the one you're looking for."

"Yea, you're the one. I don't give a shit how much you deny it. You always swear to God that you're innocent. I know you better than you know yourself. So, this is what's about to happen. You're going to take us to the products you stole from the warehouse. After that, you get out of town and stay out of town, unless you want to be the last member of your family still breathing."

Fast Lane didn't budge, "How can I give you something I don't have, Bird? You're not making sense."

JayBird was done talking, "Ace, go get the boy." I was hoping it wouldn't come down to that, but it was the only way Fast Lane would bend. He would rather let you take his life than get caught in a lie.

Fast Lane's son was fast asleep when I got him out of bed and walked him to the living room. He was still wiping the sleep from his eyes when he saw his father sitting in a chair in the middle of the living. The boy tried to run to his daddy, but I held him back.

The boy struggled and started to cry out, "Daddy!"

Raquel was scared but tried not escalate the situation. "Please, don't hurt my baby," she pleaded trying to hold back tears.

"We won't, as long as Fast Lane gives what we want," I said while cocking the hammer on my .38. The child screamed, and I covered his mouth with my hand.

"Just give them what they want. Please! It's not worth it, Lane," Raquel cried out more dramatic that time.

Fast Lane reluctantly gave in. "Fine, it was me. I broke in the warehouse with my homies, and we took everything, but I didn't kill nobody. I swear. You can have it all back. Just don't hurt my son."

"That wasn't so hard now was it?" asked JayBird. We stood him up and started to walk him out the front door.

"Can y'all at least cut the ties off? I can't feel my hands." JayBird thought about it before telling James to cut the restraints.

"Try something, and I'll put a bullet in your ass, Lane," said James as he cut the zip tie off. Lane rubbed his wrists to get the blood to circulate through the numbness.

JayBird turned to Raquel before we walked out and said, "Sorry for the inconvenience, Ms. You have a good night." Then, he threw her a wad of cash for cooperating. She caught it and looked at him, unsure if she should say thank you or you're welcome.

We kept Fast Lane close to us as we exited the house and walked down the driveway passing Fast Lane's car. When we reached the gate, we heard two car doors open behind us. Shots were being fired from both sides of the car as two men shot at us from inside the car. We all dove out of harm's way. The engine roared awake, and the car's tires screeched and sent the car into reverse.

We scattered as the car swerved into the street and the passenger door flung open. Fast Lane managed to push me off of him, and I lost my footing as I connected with the concrete. "Get the fuck off me!" The rage in his voice was almost demonic when he said, "Next time, I'll shoot to kill, bitch!" The words rang out in my ears as he dove head first into the car, and they sped off with the door still ajar.

"Son of a bitch," hollered JayBird "Let's get 'em." JayBird's goons took off after the car before us, but we weren't far behind when our SUV swerved out of the parking spot in pursuit of Fast Lane's car.

The roads were occupied with light traffic as we saw Fast Lane's car dip in and out of lanes and into oncoming traffic to avoid being held up. We tried to keep up, but the SUV's were no match for the custom-built turbo engine. Fast Lane was so far ahead of us. We saw him stop the car to jump out of the passenger seat and into the driver seat.

We were nearly on his tail again when Fast Lane punched the gas to catch the traffic light before it turned red, but his timing was off and the light changed before he cleared the crosswalk. Fast Lane looked up into the rearview to see how far behind we were when an eighteen wheeler commercial truck smashed into the front end of his car and sent it spinning to the opposite end of intersection before come to a halt.

Passersby pulled over and ran towards the wreck, but the car instantaneously burst into flames, followed by an explosion that sent the good Samaritans running for cover. We watched the car burn from a distance. They had no chance of surviving the crash.

"Damn! That's one hundred grand I'll never see again," said JayBird as he watched without blinking, like the car was a pile of burning money.

"Fast Lane was the one who shot me. He told me he was going to "shoot to kill" next time before he pushed me off him and jumped in the car."

They all looked at me, trying to wrap their minds around the strange chain of events that we just experienced. None of us wanted to say it, but there was a reason Fast Lane and his thugs didn't make it across that intersection.

VIII

The scene of Fast Lane's car engulfed in flames and black smoke still burned in my brain after we got back to JayBird's warehouse that night. The fact that the people who were responsible for trying to kill me were no more was liberating, but it still did not change the fact Cloud 9 and C-Note were murdered in cold blood just to send me a message. I was experiencing a guilt trip more than a victorious one.

Cloud 9 and C-Note had nothing to do with my beef with Fast Lane, nor did I know he was trying to destroy the empire I worked so hard to build. When the pieces of the puzzle came together, the picture was disturbing, but the mystery was solved and valuable lessons were learned: Your enemies may be out of sight and mind, but that doesn't mean you are out of theirs.

JayBird was furious when he entered the warehouse and kicked over a stack of boxes. James, Black, and I followed behind him as the sound of fragile items breaking upon contact with the floor echoed throughout the warehouse. In all the years I've known JayBird, he never displayed that type of out of control temper around me.

The only time I saw him get upset was when he had to get into employees' asses about poor job performance. That was nothing compared to what we were witnessing. JayBird swung his office door open hard and punched a hole- the size of the doorknob- into the drywall.

JayBird pounded his fists on his desk three times, still trying to release his anger. I tried to calm him down before he blew a blood vessel in his brain.

"Yo, Bird, I know you're mad about your money, but at least you don't have to worry about Lane popping up again to start something. We lost soldiers to this shit, and they didn't have anything to do with that beef. You can make the money back, but Nine and Note, we can't get them back."

JayBird was breathing heavy, and his forehead was covered in beads of sweat when he looked at me and said, "I fucked up by letting him walk away from here the first time. All of this could have been avoided if I took care of that punk bitch when he got over on me for forty grand. Now, I'm out one hundred grand and innocent lives were lost. And, he tried to take others. If I'm mad at anything, I'm mad at myself for not acting when I should have."

JayBird's panting started to return to normal breathing as he leaned on the edge of his desk and wiped the sweat from his forehead. I walked over to him and put a hand on his shoulder.

"Come on, Bird. You didn't make him steal from you. You didn't make him run, and you didn't make him or his thugs come after my squad. You can't blame yourself for the actions of others, Boss. I know you're not used to taking a loss, but the only thing to do now is rebuild."

"You're right, Ace," sighed JayBird. "Gotta keep it moving." JayBird took a seat in his chair behind the desk and asked, "Fellas, you mind giving Ace and me a moment to talk? Help yourself to whatever you want in the kitchen. This won't take long."

"Not a problem, Bird," said Black, before leaving the room with James.

"Sit down, Ace. I wanna talk to you for a min," said JayBird as I sat in one of the chairs on the other side of the desk.

"What's on your mind?" I asked, wondering what he wanted to discuss without James or Black in the room.

"First of all, I wanna give you your props, Ace," explained JayBird. "You've been down from day one, and I've never had any problems with you. Yeah, you were the youngest on my roster, but you're the only one I could trust in the office and in the lab. Then, you became my best client when you left the nest and took over the west side with your team and came up faster than a balloon full of helium. If I said anything bad about you, I'd be lying. I'd be dead if it weren't for you."

JayBird's words made me feel like I was about to be presented with an award of excellence at the end of his speech. No one had ever acknowledged my accomplishments. Whether you agreed with my career choice or not, it took a lot of hard work to get to where I was, and no one could take that from me.

"Thanks, Jay. I know better than to bite the hand that fed me. You gave me an opportunity, and I ran with it. Now, here I am today, about to open my own business after everything I've been through. I guess you can say we saved each other's lives," I said expressing my gratitude for JayBird's praise.

"You're right. We did save each other, and that's what I want to talk to you about," JayBird said as he shifted in his chair before continuing. "I know you said you were ready to retire from the game, but I've been thinking about the recent turn of events, and I came to the conclusion that you're not ready to move on."

I raised an eyebrow involuntarily from the confusion that took over my thoughts. "What do you mean I'm not ready, Jay? I made the decision to call it quits. I thought about it long and hard, and this life ain't for me anymore. I'm hanging it up."

JayBird was noticeably unsatisfied with my reply as he shifted in his chair again and made the leather speak from friction. He was straightforward without candy-coating his words.

"Let me put it this way. I'm not ready for you to quit yet. I just took a loss that is going to take time to recover from, and seeing that you're my best client, Ace, I still need you on the roster."

"I understand you took a loss, but I'm not the one who robbed you, Jay. This part of my life is over," I protested. "Nothing and no one can make me stay in the game another day. I'm on another path now, and I'm not turning back. That's all there is to it."

"No, that's not all there is to it, Ace." JayBird was unhappy with my defiance. "Did you forget who put you on?" I chose not to respond to the rhetorical question. I folded my arms across my chest and leaned back in the chair, preparing myself for a debate.

"The way I see it, you wouldn't have shit if it wasn't for me. All that money you're investing into the club was made with my products, the products that I let you have at a discount, unlike any of my other clients." JayBird's tone was confrontational. "Like you said, Ace. You can't bite the hand that feeds you, and I feel you nibbling at my fingertips. I've always treated you like family, and now you wanna run out on me when I need you to hold it down?"

"Look, I appreciate everything you've done for me, Jay, but my life is more important than this money. Yeah, I don't have to worry about Fast Lane anymore, but how do I know there's not some other hater out there who will put a gun to my head just to take over my territory or rob me like they got you?" I was purposely being stubborn as a bull. "Sorry, but my mind is made up. After the trials I faced and overcame, I'm lucky to be alive. I've been burned once, and I'm not playing with fire again. Next time, I might not be so lucky, and no one, not even you is going to be there to help me. I still got your back if you ever need me, but I can't help you like that."

JayBird's nostrils flared open widely as he tried to react to my resistance in a civilized manner. "I hate that it has to come to this. I'm going to give you a couple of options to choose from, and I'll let you sleep on it before getting back to me. You can either 1) keep hustling with your team until I've recouped my losses, including a severance to make sure my empire doesn't take another loss after you're gone. Or, you can 2) give me a percentage of ownership and make me a partner at the club until I've recovered from my losses just as the first option. The choice is yours. You have until tomorrow to figure it out."

That was a side of JayBird I never knew existed. The way he was talking to me sounded foreign to my ears, but I replied with a question: "And what if I don't stay with the team and keep hustling or give you a percentage of the club? What are you going to do, huh?"

"I'm sorry, Ace. Did you forget I know everything about you? Just know you brought it upon yourself, but I will ruin everything you've worked for," rebutted JayBird. "I'm sure the feds would love to know where you got the money to invest into a club. Wouldn't they? I know you don't want to see years of hard earned money confiscated while they put you behind bars. Right?" JayBird seemed like a completely different person.

"So, you're going to try and pull this shit on me of all people?"

JayBird disregarded my question when he said, "You have twenty-four hours to decide; no more, no less."

There was no negotiating with JayBird when he had an idea in his head. I just couldn't believe he would blackmail me when all I've done was be loyal and fill his wallet up with cash. I was doing the dirty work while he watched from a distance and gave orders, hardly ever getting his hands dirty. JayBird's eyes were empty when I gave him a blank stare to study the unknown personality I was dealing with.

As I walked out of his office, I said, "Maybe some of what Fast Lane said was true. Just know I'm not one of your bitches on a leash." JayBird smirked like he was going to reply, but I was already out of the door descending the staircase.

Black and James waited for me at the bottom of the staircase. I passed them and said, "Let's get the fuck out of here." The two of them noticed my attitude was on edge.

James tried to get answers. "Yo, Ace, you good, bruh? What happened up there?"

"I'll tell y'all later. Now is not the time." I explained while trying to get out of the front door as fast as possible. I was experiencing more emotions than I knew how to express at the moment. Mostly, I was in shock from what JayBird just told me.

As Black pulled away from the warehouse, I collected my thoughts in the backseat. I didn't want to tell James and Black about JayBird trying to blackmail me. They would have wanted to go back and have a little discussion with JayBird, but I wanted to make sure nothing would stop me from opening the club. I needed to figure out how I was going to deal with JayBird myself.

I told Black to drop me off at the condo; then, I asked the both of them to stop and relay the news about Fast Lane to the rest of the team. They were still on standby and ready for a call to action, so the team would be relieved to know we took care of our problem, even though all of them had no idea who Fast Lane was. All they needed to know was we were no longer at war with the army of ghosts.

The team was ready to get back to business as usual, and I told James to tell them we were clear to start making moves again, as long as they didn't roll solo. Fast Lane was dead, but we still needed to be cautious about who we were dealing with.

Black dropped me off at the condo and kept pushing towards the team. Everything was happening so fast, and I needed a chance to be alone with my thoughts, to make sense of all of the mayhem around me and my team. Fast Lane and his homies deserved what they got when that semi-truck sent them into the afterlife in the blink of an eye. There wasn't a square inch in my body that felt sympathy for them. The only reason I wished one of them lived was to show JayBird where the stash of products was hidden, so he wouldn't blackmail me to help him recover the loss.

The silence at the condo was meant to help me sort the many thoughts that were running through my mind at once, but the silence was louder than I could take. I needed to get out and have a drink to relax, so I drove downtown to find a place where I could throw back a few cold ones.

I managed to make my way into a jazz club, where a five-piece band was making the place alive with the sound of music as I made my way to the bar to order a brew. The mug was in my hand just as fast as the bartender sat it down, and it was in my stomach about the same speed it took for him to fill the mug. I tapped the mug on the bar to signal that I needed another.

As the jazz band played, I stared down into my mug, as if I was trying to count the amount of bubbles in my drink, but my mind was in another place as I absorbed the music. I was lost in thought until I felt a hand on my shoulder and heard a female's voice say, "Ace, what are you doing here?"

I looked up and saw Lisette smiling at me as I said, "Just felt like stepping out and having a drink for a moment. That's all."

"I see. I never expected to see you in a place like this," she said while waving the bartender over. "Long Island Ice Tea, please."

"Yeah, I actually just chose this place randomly, but it's nice," I said while taking another sip of beer.

The bartender served a frosty beverage to Lisette as she sat down in the chair next to me. I tried not to stare, but Lisette was wearing a red dress that hugged every curve of her body. I couldn't help but to take an extended glance at her before refocusing my eyes elsewhere.

Lisette took a sip of her drink, then asked, "So, what's wrong? Everything okay?"

"Yea, of course. I'm fine," I lied to avoid further investigation. "Why do you ask?"

Lisette took another sip of her cocktail and said, "Because when I got here, I saw you staring into your mug like you lost something important in there."

I couldn't help but to laugh at the fact that she picked up my vibe. "Okay, I guess you can read me a little better than I tried to disguise it."

"Well, it's not that hard to stand out when you're the only one staring at the beer in your mug instead of watching the band play," said Lisette.

I looked around to see that I was indeed the only one who wasn't watching the show. "Okay, you got me on that too."

Lisette swirled the straw around in her glass and said, "So, I'm guessing you don't want to talk about it? I already told you I'm here for you if you want to talk. We're going to be working together for a long time, so you might as well tell me anything that I need to know about you now."

She took another sip of her cocktail, and I watched her full lips painted in red surround the straw to drink. I must have been momentarily hypnotized because when she looked up, my eyes were fixated a little too long, and she caught me staring. Lisette smiled when I looked away like a grade-schooler. She had caught me in the act, and there was no denying it.

"See, that's exactly why I can't talk to you. How am I supposed to talk about what's bothering me when I can't even think of what the problem is when you're in front of me?"

She spun her barstool around and put her back towards me saying, "Is that better?"

I laughed at her sarcasm. "Well, if you were looking at what I'm looking at you probably wouldn't consider it better."

She swiftly spun the stool around and said, "Were you looking at my booty, you pervert?"

I answered honestly, "I never told you to spin around. That was your idea. Can't get mad at me."

Lisette laughed, "I don't know what I'm going to do with you, sir. You're going to be trouble." Our eyes connected, and I could feel the electricity flowing between us.

"You should join me, and we can be troublemakers together," I suggested.

Lisette was curious, "What do you mean by 'troublemakers'?"

I took a chance and leaned in to softly kiss Lisette's plump red lips; then, I pulled back. Our eyes connected again. Both of us could feel the sexual energy flowing as Lisette leaned back in and kissed me again with more passion as her tongue entered my mouth and teased mine, gently biting my bottom lip as she pulled away. My eyes were still closed momentarily after the kiss still feeling the tingly sensation that ran through my body.

When I opened my eyes again, Lisette was staring at me in my eyes with a seductive smile and said, "So, that's what you mean by troublemakers. I think I like that." I gently slid my hand up her thigh starting from her knee, then back down again.

"Maybe, we should be troublemakers somewhere else."

Lisette scrunched her lips together as if she was in deep consideration of what I was suggesting. "You know, I live a couple of blocks away from here, and I've got a bottle of wine that I've been dying to try. Maybe you can come and help me with it?"

My heart skipped a beat when she asked me to join her at her place for a drink. "I think I can help you with that. I mean I wouldn't want you to be forced to drink that whole bottle by yourself," I said before finishing off the rest of my beer. Lisette finished her drink, and we left the club as the jazz band continued to entertain the full house of guests.

The city air was crisp that night, and I grabbed ahold of Lisette's hand, as we walked a few blocks over to a plush sky-scraper in the heart of downtown and took the elevator up to the eighteenth floor.

When we got to Lisette's unit, she opened the door and revealed an upscale luxury apartment with contemporary furniture and glass walls that showed a view of the city that only the privileged get to witness on a daily basis. I walked over to the window and looked down at the cars zipping down the freeway and said, "Nice view."

"You like that, Ace?" She asked as I continued to gaze down at the city lights. "What about this view?"

I turned around and saw Lisette's silhouette across the room, as she walked towards me and the glow of blue light from the full moon that entered through the windows of the apartment revealed her bare body. The sight of her goddess body, her full round breasts, small waist and curvy hips took my breath away as I gasped for air and said, "I like this view too. As a matter of fact, I love this view."

Lisette approached me, and I kissed her as I wrapped my arms around her waist. I slid my hands down and cuffed her round soft skin in the palms of my hands, as I felt blood rush to middle of my body. She unbuckled my belt and unbuttoned my pants. As they dropped to the floor, Lisette felt me with her hands, and I moaned as I gently caressed her neck with my tongue. I picked up Lisette, and she wrapped her legs around my waist as I walked back towards her couch, kissing her with her tongue circling around mine.

I laid her down on the couch and pulled my shirt off in the same motion and continued to kiss her, moving down to her breasts as she let out a deep moan. I slid my hand down and felt Lisette was dripping wet. She wrapped her legs around my waist, and as I slid inside of her, she moaned, pushing me deeper inside of her, while thrusting her waist forward.

I made love to Lisette until we both exploded with pleasure. She cried out from the intense stimulation, as I looked at her deeply in her eyes. Still feeling the over-whelming sensation running through my body, I collapsed on top of Lisette as we both tried to catch our breath. I didn't feel myself dose off, as we both fell asleep without moving an inch.

The morning sun shined through the window and stopped me from sleeping. When I woke up, I was covered in a blanket and lying on the couch by myself. The aroma of freshly ground coffee being brewed filled the apartment as I blinked my eyes rapidly to focus and wiped the crust from the corner of my eyes. I looked around the apartment trying to find Lisette when she emerged from the bathroom in a robe with steam from the hot shower following her. She looked over at the couch and saw me looking at her and said, "Oh, the troublemaker is awake. Good morning."

I flopped back down on the couch and laughed, "Yea, barely. But, I'm up. And it's a great morning waking up to your beautiful self."

Lisette giggled as she walked into the kitchen to pour herself a cup of coffee, "Do you drink coffee, Ace?"

I got up from the couch and started to walk over to her and said, "Usually not, but I'll take a cup. We got a big day today."

Lisette poured a cup of coffee for me and walked over while saying, "Yes, we have to meet Mr. Weils at the club in about two hours to see the final touches on the remodeling and to sign the rest of the paperwork."

"I still can't believe it's actually about to happen," I said while slowly sipping the hot beverage.

"Well, you better start believing really soon, Ace," said Lisette as she mixed a little more sugar into her coffee. "We cut the ribbon next week. Then, we're open for business, and there's no turning back at that point. And while we're on the subject, let's keep what happened last night between us. We don't need Mr. Weils to know about us. Let's keep it strictly business in front of him for now okay, Ace?"

I nodded my head to agree. "Fine by me. So, guess that means I'll meet you at the club in couple hours then?" Lisette unwrapped her hair from the towel and let it fall as she walked towards me and gave me a peck on the lips.

Then, she walked to her room to get ready for the day ahead of us while saying, "You know how to let yourself out right? Take your time with the coffee. I'm going to get dressed, and I'll see you in a few."

After finishing the coffee, I left Lisette's apartment with a smile plastered across my face and made my way back to the condo to prepare for the meeting with Derek.

When I arrived to the club, Lisette and Derek were waiting for me to arrive, as they met me at the front entrance to invite me inside. The club smelled brand new, and I was pleased to see a beautifully constructed club with modern furniture and decor for the sophisticated adult crowd that we were planning to appeal to.

A few construction workers were still there working on the final touches of the remodeling when I walked inside and looked over our investment. Derek put a hand on my shoulder and asked, "Well, what do you think, Ace? Beautiful isn't it?"

I set my eyes upon the establishment without blinking and said, "That does not even begin to describe what I'm seeing."

"Good; I'm glad you like it. Come right this way. One more week, Ace, and we'll be open for business. I just need your auto-graph on a few more documents, and we'll be good to go," said Derek as he directed me to a table where he had paperwork out ready to be signed.

Derek handed me a pen, and I began to sign off on documents when my cell phone rang. I looked at my phone, and my stomach turned when I saw 'JayBird' on the caller ID.

"I'm sorry, Mr. Weils. I need to take this call," I said excusing myself from the table. I then walked into an area with more privacy to talk to JayBird alone. I answered the phone and before I could say hello JayBird said, "So, what's it going to be, Ace? I went by the club earlier, and it looks real nice. I'd hate for you to have to lose your investment over something so small."

JayBird was making me angry, but I tried to keep my voice low so Derek and

Lisette wouldn't hear me arguing from across the empty club.

I don't know what came over me, but I was fed up with JayBird trying to push me around. I decided right then and there that it was my life and my decision. Even though he had done a lot for me in the past, I could not let JayBird dictate my future because there was no telling how far he would go. I refused JayBird's offer.

"You know what, Bird? I'm going to tell you like I told you before. I'm done with the game, and I'm done with you."

"You sure about that, Ace? Don't be stupid," challenged JayBird.

"I've done more than enough for you, Jay. I don't owe you anything. I'm not going to be your scapegoat forever. Solve your own fucking problems. I'm done," I said before hanging the phone up in JayBird's face.

Telling JayBird to go fuck himself never felt better. I felt like a free man as I walked back over to Derek and Lisette with a smile of confidence as I said, "Now where were we before we were so rudely interrupted?" Lisette pointed at one of the documents I was about to sign. "You left off right here, Mr. Johnson."

When I finished signing paperwork, I went to have a celebratory dinner with Derek and Lisette. Then, I went back to the condo to wait for Black and James to meet me there. They needed to know what JayBird was trying to do, so we could plan how we were going to go about stopping the situation from escalating. When I walked into the condo that night, I received a call from an unknown number. I answered the phone, and the voice on the other end spoke in urgency, "Hello is this Amir Johnson?"

I answered, "Yes," and the voice continued, "This is Sgt. Hall, Arson Investigator. Sir, we have you listed as one of the owners of 1423 N. Broadway. The property was severely damaged in a fire that occurred just over an hour ago. We need you to come down to the scene to answer some questions, please."

IX

The stench of charred building materials invaded my nostrils as I pulled up and parked outside of what used to be my club and future. Two fire engines and several unmarked fire and police cruisers were parked in front of the building, as firefighters worked to clear the sidewalk of debris, and arson investigators and detectives studied the remains of the club for clues. The sight of my investment being demolished a week before our grand opening made me nauseous. I tried to hold my composure as I got out of the car and approached the scene.

Yellow caution tape surrounded the perimeter of the building. Most of the exterior structure was still standing, but the renovations inside were completely destroyed. Everything that was flammable was burned to ashes. I went to duck under the caution tape when one of the firefighters stopped me in my tracks and said, "Sir, this area is off limits to the public right now. I'm going to have to ask you to step back on the other side of the yellow tape."

"I'm one of the owners of this club," I explained as I continued to walk towards the scene. "I need to speak with Investigator Hall."

The firefighter put his arm out to block my path, then gave me an order: "Wait right here. This is an open investigation. If any of the evidence is tampered with, the case could be altered and possibly kill our chances of finding the arsonist. So if you want answers, I'd suggest you wait right here while I find Hall."

I crossed my arms across my chest to try and contain myself from losing my temper. The firefighter had no idea that my life was spiraling out of control day by day, so I tried not to take my anger out on him. I shrugged my shoulders and said, "I'm waiting."

Whether the evidence was sufficient enough to find out who burned the club down or not, I already knew who was responsible; even if JayBird did not spark the flame himself, he was still the number one suspect. JayBird hardly got his hands dirty, so I was certain that he sent a couple of his goons to carry out the terrorist act. They were all professionals and catching them would not be easy because they paid attention to details and covered their tracks to the point of nonexistence.

JayBird's goons would never snitch if they were to get caught up with the authorities, so finding out who set the club on fire would mean nothing in the long run if the person who hired them was still walking the streets as a free man.

The firefighter who stopped me from entering the building stepped out of the burnt remains escorting a middle-aged man with salt and pepper hair wearing a navy blue windbreaker jacket that had *ARSON* printed in bold yellow letters on both sides.

"You must be Mr. Johnson. I'm Arson Investigator Hall," his voice was authoritative as he extended his hand to firmly shake mine. I tried my best to greet Investigator Hall properly.

"I'd like to say it's nice to meet you, but I would be lying. No offense."

Investigator Hall was quick to reassure me, "None taken. If I were you, I wouldn't want to meet me under these circumstances either. But I know what you're going through, and I'm only here to help." I was appreciative of Investigator Hall's understanding.

"You're just a man doing his job. All I can do is thank you."

Investigator Hall motioned for me to follow him and said, "Step into my office." I followed him through the blackened entrance as he gave instructions. "Stay next to me. Don't wander off, and don't touch anything because it may be evidence, and you'll fuck this case up if you tamper with it. So keep your hands to yourself, or in your pockets. Just don't touch shit."

I raised my hands innocently. "Got it. I'm in a strip club."

When I laid my eyes upon the destructtion, I felt my blood pressure rise and my heart rate quicken. I tried to control my sudden heavy breathing and said, "We didn't even get a chance to open our doors for business. The grand opening was supposed to be next week. The fountain was going to be installed in the morning. We would have been good to go after that."

Investigator Hall looked at me and said, "So that explains why the sprinkler system didn't activate. That would have saved your club from being completely destroyed. You may have had to deal with the water damage, but your property could have been salvaged."

I shook my head from disbelief, "Perfect timing."

Investigator Hall turned towards me and asked, "Do you have any enemies, Mr. Johnson?" The question he threw at me was a complicated one, but I gave the smartest answer I could think of.

"Nope. Not that I know of. Why do you ask?"

"Well, so far we determined that the fire was started using Molotov cocktails," answered Investigator Hall, "but we have not determined how many were used to start the fire. When taking into consideration how fast the building burned, there had to be at least three arsonists involved to deliver the amount of gasoline needed to burn a structure of this size before the fire department responded."

What Investigator Hall said made perfect sense, as I already expected JayBird had sent his goons to do his dirty work.

Steering the investigation towards JayBird would have been useless, because he was the general, and he sent his soldiers on the mission. There was no way to be sure who he sent.

My hands weren't squeaky clean either, and if JayBird were to go down, I know he would find a way to take me with him or send some goons to let my family feel the wrath of my endeavors gone wrong. Because that wasn't an option, I had to figure out how to deal with that on my own. I lied to Investigator Hall, but there was a good reason for my dishonesty.

"I wish I knew who would do something like this, but if I think of anything that might help, I will contact you."

"Please do. Sometimes, it's the people you least expect, and sometimes it's just a random act of stupidity by some pyromaniac looking for a thrill," said Investigator Hall. "You have insurance right?"

"Yes, sir. My partner, Mr. Weils, should have the policy information at the office. I've been trying to contact him, but I haven't been able to get in touch with him yet. He is going to flip when he finds out this happened."

The firefighter who stopped me at the door walked up behind us and said, "Excuse me, sir. There are a couple of guys outside saying you're expecting them."

James and Black had finally shown up, and we had a lot to discuss, so I asked Investigator Hall if we were done for the time being. He gave me his card and urged me to call him if I had any questions or concerns and said he would be in touch within the next couple of days to follow up with me.

When I stepped outside, James and Black stood behind the caution tape. As soon as Black saw me, he blurted out, "Yo, how did this happen, Ace?"

We greeted each with a half handshake and half hug, as I replied, "Come on. Let's roll out, and I'll put y'all up on game. We gotta make some moves." I hopped in the backseat when we got into Black's SUV and said, "Don't drive off yet. I need to talk to y'all first." Black turned the engine off and then the radio as both of them turned an open ear towards me.

James asked, "What's the deal, Ace? Talk to us."

"When JayBird wanted to talk to me alone the other night before we left the warehouse, he came at me with some foul shit. Long story short- he's trying to blackmail me and the team. Since he took that loss from Fast Lane, he wants the team to keep hustling until he recovers from his losses, plus the time it will take to earn a nest egg to fall back on in case he takes another loss when we quit the game. Or, he wants fifty percent of my cut of the club money once we're open for business, until he recovers from the loss. We're his number one clients, and he's trying to keep that cash flowing as long as possible."

"Man, fuck that." Black didn't like what he was hearing. "We don't owe that nigga shit! That shit Fast Lane pulled had nothing to do with us. We took a loss that we will never recover from, and he's worried about his money? Hope you told him to get the fuck outta here with that nonsense, Ace. He got the wrong ones."

"You know I did." I felt my temperature rise as I continued. "But then he said he would get the feds involved and shut down the club because I'm using drug money to start the business, and if I try to snitch on him, he'll put a price on my mom's head. He said he'd let me sleep on it, but when he called me I told him to solve his own fucking problems."

Black turned and looked at me with pride and said, "That's what I'm talking 'bout, Ace. If that nigga Bird wants conflict, we got that for 'em."

James wasn't as pumped up as Black, but his nose was turned up and his mouth was twisted when he said, "So, you think he's the one who set the club on fire?"

There was not a doubt in my mind that JayBird was responsible for the fire, but since I had no real proof I answered, "No, I don't think he set the club on fire, but I do think he sent some of his goons to do the dirty work. He said he would drop dime on me to the feds, but he probably was just trying to scare me into doing what he wanted. By burning down the club, I would have no choice but to get back in the game until I recover from the loss. He's trying to manipulate the situation, and if I confront him about it, he will never admit it."

"Why don't you call him and see what he says," suggested James. "See what his attitude about the situation is like? We shouldn't go looking for him just yet. Shit can escalate and pop off real quick, and none of us need blood on our hands. If we're going to deal with JayBird, we gotta be smart about it."

James was right. If I confronted JayBird face to face, we might start something that could end in bloodshed. I never thought JayBird would be someone that I would have conflict with. If anything, he was one of the people in my life that I could count on to have my back without question.

But now that his true colors are exposed, he will never be able to camouflage himself again. The only thing JayBird cared about more than anything was money, and if you came between him and money in any way, you were a problem that needed to be addressed. JayBird doesn't stop until he gets what he wants, so I would have to think like him if I wanted to free myself from the madness because the problem wasn't going to disappear.

I took out my cell phone and dialed JayBird's number. He sounded delighted that I was calling him when he answered and said, "So, you finally came to your senses. I knew you would see things my way sooner or later."

"Get over yourself, Bird. That's not why I called," my demeanor was cold.

JayBird chuckled under his breath and said, "If you're not calling me about making this money, you should hang up now. We have nothing else to talk about, Ace."

My jaw clenched together to keep me from losing my cool. I was straightforward with him when I said, "Yea, we got something to talk about. My club was set on fire tonight. We lost everything. You're taking this too far, Bird. I've always done right by you."

JayBird denied my accusation and calmly replied, "I don't know what you're talking about, Ace. I had nothing to do with that. But while we're on the subject, you should let that teach you a lesson about how karma works. Remember when we were talking about biting the hand that feeds you? All I was asking of you was to help me out of a situation, and you turned your back on me after everything that I've done for you and your team. You're barking up the wrong tree if you think I was involved in what happened to your club. That was karma biting you back for your lack of loyalty."

Everything JayBird said sounded like a bullshit tactic to justify why he had a legitimate reason to destroy my future plans. I disregarded everything JayBird said as fast as the words left his mouth and said, "Fuck what you're talking about Bird. Somebody threw enough cocktails at my club to destroy everything before the fire department could get there, and right now, you're the number one suspect, even if you didn't do the dirty work."

JayBird was growing agitated as he growled, "Like I said the first time, if you're not calling me to talk about making this money, you should put the phone down. But seeing that you need an income now, I'm sure you won't mind changing the subject. Just let me know when you're ready."

I smirked at JayBird's arrogance and replied, "You'll die an old man from natural causes before I fuck with you again. I'm not making no more deals with the devil."

JayBird managed to say, "We'll see," before I hung up in his face.

I threw the phone down into the seat next to me and buried my face in my hands as James said, "That son of a bitch knows something; motha' fucka' talks like he's invincible. Did he forget you saved his life? That act alone is worth more than anything he's ever done for you or the team."

"Fuck it. We'll get back to him later. It's more important that we need to get in contact with Mr. Weils. He still doesn't know what happened tonight," I said while straightening my posture and grabbing my phone off the seat. I dialed Derek's cell phone, and it went straight to voicemail without ringing.

The office number also answered with the after-business hour's voicemail. "His phone is still dead. I know it's past midnight, but this isn't like Mr. Weils. That man is always on call," I concluded before dialing Lisette's number. Lisette's phone rang several times before the voicemail answered for her; I called her two more times for good measure before giving up.

"Come on. Let's go to Lisette's apartment. She's just a few blocks away from here," I said while strapping on my seatbelt. "This can't wait until tomorrow." The engine roared as Black started the SUV and pulled off towards Lisette's building without hesitation.

Black and James waited for me in the car while I went up to Lisette's apartment. Good thing the guard recognized me from the night before when I went home with Lisette, because she didn't answer the phone when he called her to approve access to the building. I told the guard about the emergency, and she recited the residency policy, "Well, technically, I'm not supposed to let you up without approval, but seeing that Lisette couldn't shut up about you when she came home tonight, I doubt it will be a problem. I just need to see your I.D. then you can go up and try your luck ringing the doorbell instead of her phone."

I thanked the guard with a tip even though she tried to refuse the money. I ran into the elevator before she could give it back to me. When I got up to Lisette's apartment, I rang the doorbell three times and waited. After ringing the bell again, I heard Lisette's house slippers slide across the floor with each step she took towards the door and her drowsy voice say, "This better be important."

Lisette's voice turned up a few notches when she looked through the peephole and saw me standing on the other side of the door. "Ace, what are you doing here? Do you know what time it is?" Lisette opened the door and let me in.

I wasted no time trying to explain, "My bad. I called you a few times, but you didn't answer, and it's an emergency. The club caught fire tonight. Everything was burned to ashes."

Lisette's eyes stretched wide open, and she gasped for air then shouted, "What?! How the hell did that happen?"

"Arson, molotov cocktails," I tried to explain as quickly as possible. "The sprinkler system never activated because we shut off the water for that fountain installation."

"I can't believe my ears. This is unreal," said Lisette as she sat down on the couch to absorb the impact of the bad news.

"I've been trying to call Derek, for the past couple of hours, but his cell keeps going straight to voicemail," I said as I took a seat next to Lisette on the couch.

"That's weird. He never turns his phone off," said Lisette, "And if it dies, it's not dead for long because he's on the clock twenty-four hours a day. I can't tell you how many times he awakened me in the middle of the night about work. It happens at least once a week."

The matter was urgent, and Derek needed to be notified immediately, so I asked Lisette, "Where does he live?"

"He lives in a gated community out in the suburbs," she explained. "I'll go with you. The sensor for the gate is on my car. That way you don't have to get clearance from the gate guard since he's not picking up the phone."

"I'm ready when you are," I said as Lisette went to her bedroom to grab a sweatshirt and her purse before leaving for Derek's house.

I rode with Lisette, while Black and James followed closely behind us until we arrived to the gated community that was nestled in the foothills of the suburban neighborhood on the outskirts of the city. Once we exited the freeway, we traveled up a lonely road for a couple of miles before arriving to the towering gates that secured the front entrance of the gated community.

Black followed closely behind us as we pulled up to the automatic resident's entrance and waited for the gate to open automatically.

When the gate failed to budge, Lisette crept a few feet closer and tapped the sensor in case it was malfunctioning. "What is wrong with this thing? I've never had a problem getting in. Maybe there's something wrong with the gate," said Lisette as she put the car in reverse and pulled up to the guard shack at the entrance.

The guard muted the volume on the television before standing up to assist us and asked, "How can I help you this evening?" The elderly guard wore bifocal lenses and his perfectly groomed hair was all white and sat on his head like a helmet.

Lisette smiled at the guard and started to explain, "Is there something wrong with the resident's gate? I'm Mr. Weils' personal assistant, and I tried to go through, but the gate never opened for me. Maybe it's the sensor?"

"The gate has been working fine all night," said the guard before walking over to look at the sensor in the top left hand corner of the windshield. "Let's check the status of your sensor on the computer." The guard copied the serial numbers on a notepad and walked back into the booth.

After a couple of minutes, he walked back to the car and said, "Well, ma'am. According to the security system, your sensor was deactivated earlier today when Mr. Weils forfeited his residency with us."

Lisette unintentionally raised her voice as a natural reaction. "Forfeited? Why wouldn't he tell me he was moving!?"

"Sorry about the inconvenience Miss, but Mr. Weils hasn't been here much lately. He stopped by at the crack of dawn yesterday to drop off some paperwork and gave the movers access to his house before he left."

Lisette's expression screamed confusion as she spoke in a monotone voice. "Thanks for your help, sir."

We made a u-turn and waited for Black to pull up beside us as I relayed the news to him. "Looks like our buddy Mr. Weils moved out yesterday and failed to inform us of his plans."

"That doesn't sound right, Ace. Why would he not mention that he was moving to his personal assistant," said Black. There was no use in trying to make sense of it.

"I don't know what fuck is going on, but we have to find Derek and get to the bottom of this. Let's go check the office."

Lisette nodded to agree and said, "That's a good idea. Let's move," as we pulled onto the lonely road again.

We were still in the dark of the early morning hours when we arrived to Derek's office, a small one-story building that stands alone on its own lot. After Lisette and I got out of the car, I walked over to Black and James who were still sitting in the SUV and said, "Stay out here and keep your eyes open in case our friend Mr. Weils decides to show his face. Just honk once if you see anything. I'll be out here fast as the speed of sound."

"We got you, bruh. Our eyes are peeled," said Black, as we bumped fists before I walked towards the front door with Lisette.

The building was pitch black inside, except for the glow of the fish tank that gave life to the otherwise dull lobby. Lisette shuffled her keys around to find the right one before opening the door, but when she tried to turn the lock, it refused to open.

She let out a frustrated sigh and said, "Come on, stupid key."

"You sure you're using the right key?" I asked.

She snapped at me and said, "It's a key, not a rubix cube. I'm pretty sure I know how to use the right key to unlock a door."

I took the keys from her grip and tried to unlock the door myself before realizing, "This motherfucker changed the locks!"

"This is starting to get weirder and more confusing," said Lisette as she tried to justify the deception. "I don't know what to think at this moment, but I know that I don't like this feeling that I have right now."

"You know what? Fuck that key. I'm breaking in this bitch."

I grabbed a crowbar from Lisette's car and broke one of the small diamond shaped windows on the door and used my sleeve to unlock the door from the inside. We entered the office building using the lights on our phones to navigate through the darkness. There wasn't much time for us to search the building seeing that we were trespassing, so I went straight for Derek's office to search for some information that could help us find his whereabouts.

When I entered Derek's office, I was not prepared to see that it had been cleared. The only things he left were an empty desk and an office chair. I searched through the drawers of the desk, and the only things left were a couple of paper clips that were bent out of shape. When Black's horn suddenly honked, I sprang into action.

When I stepped back into the hallway, I heard a car start as the headlights penetrated the stained glass window on the back door. I grabbed Lisette by her arm and went for the front door.

"Come on. He has to come out of the front to leave. We'll cut him off there," I said to Lisette as we exited the front door and saw Black's SUV parked sideways in the driveway blocking Derek's path. He must have panicked when he saw us because he gunned the gas pedal and aimed for a narrow space that was too small for his luxury sedan to fit through as he rammed the back of Black's SUV and kept the pedal on the floor in an attempt to bulldoze his way to freedom.

Black hollered in anger, "Aww, this motha' fucka' done fucked up my shit. I got something for you, homie."

James looked back at Derek desperately trying to free his car. "This fool is crazy. Put it in reverse and pin him in. Don't let him get away, Black."

Black let out a war cry and switched the gears to reverse and gunned it, pinning the front end of Derek's sedan into the wall. Derek's tires screeched as he continued to hold the gas pedal down.

I took the opportunity to get him and leaped onto the roof of the car then bounced into the driveway and landed next to the driver side door. I pulled a pistol from the small of my back and smashed the window. Then, I pointed my gun at Derek and said, "Where we off to in such a hurry?"

Derek took his foot off of the gas, and I swung the door open and pulled him out of the car. I held the gun in his face with one hand and his collar with the other, pushing him against the car.

"What the fuck do you think you're doing, Mr. Weils. You trying to run out on us? Huh? After all of the money I invested in that club you thought I wasn't going to go to the ends of the Earth searching for you?" Black and James got out of the truck and walked over to assist me with roughing up Derek.

"Motha' fucka,' look at what you did to my truck," said Black as he took his anger out on Derek's face with a punch that rattled his brain as he pleaded, "Please don't kill me. I never meant for this to happen. This was not my plan. They said they would kill me if I didn't cooperate. I thought this was the only way I could get away."

"You better start making sense real soon, Weils. I don't have the time or patience for this. From what I see you were trying to disappear in the dark of the night without telling us," I said with my grip on his collar tight as a monkey wrench.

"I know this looks bad, but listen to me, Ace. Let me explain." I lowered the gun from his face but didn't release his collar.

"I'm listening."

Derek's voice calmed down as he pleaded for his life, "After we had dinner the other night, I came back to the office to get some work done, but when I got here a couple of unexpected visitors escorted me inside at gunpoint. They told me you owed them a lot of money, and if they didn't get paid, they were going to turn us into the feds because you were using laundered money to start the business. I couldn't go down like that, Ace. They were putting me in the middle of something I had nothing to do with. This one venture could have ruined me and everything I've worked for all these years. Getting out of town and cutting my losses at the club seemed like the best option. I don't want to end up in jail or dead. So, I burned down the club to cash in on the insurance. That's the only way I could think to cut my ties immediately."

I didn't waste time correcting Derek. "First off. I don't owe nobody shit. They're trying to blackmail me because I decided to quit working for them to change my life for the better. But that still doesn't explain why you were going to skip town without telling me. Whether that money was laundered or not, you were still going to cash in on the insurance and keep my cut now weren't you?"

"Ace, please," Derek asked for mercy. "I wasn't trying to get over on you intentionally. I was just scared for my life."

After thinking it over, I started to understand his take on the situation as I took my hand off of his collar and said, "See, if you would have come to me before, we could have worked something out, but I had no idea they were threatening you because they're trying to get to me. No way would I have let you suffer the consequences."

Derek knew he was wrong for assuming. "You're a good man, Ace. I'm sorry I didn't give you a chance to tell your side of the story. I'll make sure you get every penny you invested back. You have my word."

As the tension eased, I put the pistol back into the holster and said, "Both of these cars had nothing to do with this either but look at them now, innocent bystanders."

We all smiled, except for Black as he said, "Ain't shit funny about this. Look at my truck. You better come out of your pocket to get my shit fixed too, Mr. Money Bags."

Just as Derek was about to reply to Black, his voice was rendered inaudible when the sound of burning rubber screeched towards us rapidly. We turned to see another SUV swerve into the beginning of the driveway and stop, blocking all of us in. I drew my pistol again, and so did Black and James, as we anticipated the reveal of the party crashers as the blacked out windows concealed their identity.

When the doors opened, JayBird emerged from the SUV with three of his goons and said, "How come no one invited us?"

JayBird and his goons halted as James, Black, and I trained our firearms in their direction. JayBird put his hands up as his goons drew their weapons.

"Whoa, whoa, whoa. That's no way to treat a guest now is it?"

My peripheral vision caught a glimpse of Lisette ducking behind her car as I asked,

"What do you want, Bird? How did you know we were here?"

JayBird laughed and said, "All of this 'how did you find me' stuff and 'how did you know' questions. Can't you just be happy to see me?" JayBird always had access to technology that you can't get at your local electronics store. If anything, he found a way to put a bug in our phones or cars.

"I know you bugged us, you sick son of a bitch. You should get a life instead of tracking our every move."

"You call it stalking, but I call it keeping an eye on my investment," said JayBird.

JayBird's logic was fuel to the fire, and he knew it. I was done talking. "Again, what do you want, JayBird? Nobody here owes you shit, so if you're looking for money you can forget that."

JayBird wasn't hearing me as usual, "I need Mr. Weils to come with me, since you decided you're done with the streets. That insurance policy belongs to me."

"You got a hard head, Bird. Take another step, and I'm letting off the whole clip." JayBird smiled and signaled with his hand over to the other side of the building, as one of his goons that was out of view ran out and grabbed ahold of Lisette. The goon took Lisette against her will, shielding himself from our aim as he walked over to JayBird.

JayBird put his arm around Lisette and said, "Now I have something that you want. See how that works? Now all we have to do is make an even trade, and everyone walks out of here breathing and happy." There was nothing I could do. The standoff couldn't last forever, and JayBird had the upper hand.

I made promises to JayBird as I let go of Derek, "You won't get away with this, Bird. You win today, but the war ain't over. Let her go!" JayBird took his arm from around Lisette and pushed her to the ground. As she started to walk towards us, he said, "Hurry up. We ain't got all day."

I kept my gun trained on JayBird and said, "That was uncalled for, Bird. You'll get what you deserve one of these days."

JayBird smiled and said, "Not today though, Ace, not today." He hopped into the backseat of the SUV after pushing Derek inside forcefully. Once JayBird closed the door, his goons got in after him. Both sides trained our weapons on each other until their SUV pulled off and disappeared into the darkness.

About the Author

Marquez Pritchett was born in Lima, Ohio and raised in the cities of Lima and Cleveland, Ohio. Mr. Pritchett represents a new breed of writers creating young, hip and juicy street novels that give the readers a look at life from the eyes of a hustler.

Mr. Pritchett is a high school graduate of Lima Senior High School. He also attended Rhodes State College, where he majored in Business Administration. He is the creator and CEO of National Reliable Production.

Mr. Pritchett currently resides in the state of California where he is currently hard at work on his next book project.